A Midnight Miracle

A Midnight Miracle

Gary E. Parker

Revell
Grand Rapids, Michigan

Published by Fleming H. Revell
a division of Baker Publishing Group
P.O. Box 6287, Grand Rapids, MI 49516-6287

Printed in the United States of America

Library of Congress Cataloging-in-Publication Data
Parker, Gary E.
    A midnight miracle / Gary E. Parker.
        p. cm.
    ISBN 0-8007-1859-3 (cloth.)
    1. Friendship—Fiction. I. Title.
PS3566.A6784M53 2005
813'.54—dc22   2005001977

Published in association with the literary agency of Alive Communications, Inc., 7680 Goddard Street, Suite 200, Colorado Springs, CO 80920.

1

Bing Crosby crooned, "I'm dreaming of a white Christmas," through the grocery-store sound system. The smell of fruitcake and fresh pine filled the air. People pushed shopping carts full of hams, turkeys, and fixings for cranberry salad and green bean casserole and all kinds of other holiday dishes up and down the store aisles. Scores of voices chattered, threatening to drown out Crosby's music. A Christmas tree decked with red bulbs, white lights, and gold beads almost reached the ceiling near the front of the store. Electronic doors opened and closed every few seconds, and a blast of cold air jumped into the grocery each time.

Sitting at a card table about ten feet from the doors, Jenna Newsome pushed back her sandy blond hair and smiled at the old man standing on the other side of the table. She'd known Handy Jones, a mechanic who lived about three miles out of Hilltop, North Carolina, for most of her thirty years. At least twenty cakes and ten pies sat on the table between them. A stand-up poster

5

with an eight-by-eleven-inch picture of a baby boy stood behind the pies and cakes. The words "Support Mickey's Miracle" were written in bold letters above the picture.

"You want two cakes, is that right?" she asked.

Handy, dressed in worn overalls and a red baseball cap with "Chew" written on it, handed her fifty dollars. "Two ought to do real good," he said, his voice heavy with mountain twang.

"They're only fifteen apiece," Jenna said. "You spend fifty dollars on two cakes, and Martha will skin you when you get home."

Handy refused the twenty she tried to hand back. "It all goes to help Mickey, don't it?"

Jenna nodded. "Yeah. Ladies from Hilltop Community Church made and donated the cakes and pies. Every dollar we make goes to pay for Mickey's medical costs."

"Keep the change then," Handy said. "Martha won't mind. Heck, she probably made a couple of cakes herself."

"You're mighty nice," Jenna said. "Every dollar makes a difference." She pulled a brown bag from the floor, opened it, and sat the two cakes inside. A man, this one a lot younger, stepped up behind Handy.

"How much you got so far?" Handy asked.

"Not nearly enough," Jenna said. "About forty thousand dollars, and we've been at it close to two months." She glanced at the man behind Handy, and her eyes widened as she recognized Rem Lincoln. What in the world was he doing back in Hilltop?

"That's a heap of cakes to sell," Handy said.

Jenna smiled at Handy again but didn't really feel very

6

happy. "Most of the money came from donations," she said. "People didn't even get a cake."

"Folks around here got good hearts."

She handed Handy the bag and tried to stay positive but found it tough. As the chair of a group raising money for a bone marrow transplant for a baby boy with no health insurance, she knew better than anybody that things didn't look good.

"How much you got to raise?" Handy asked.

Rem shifted, and Jenna thought he was going to leave without speaking. Maybe he didn't recognize her.

"Close to two hundred fifty thousand," she said, her eyes still on Rem. "Within the next couple of weeks too. If we don't get it by then, it might be too late."

"You needin' a miracle, I reckon."

"You can say that again. Say hello to Martha for me."

Handy tipped his hat and stepped away. Rem moved to the table, and Jenna sat up straighter without quite knowing why. Rem wore khaki pants, a chocolate-brown V-neck sweater, a navy waist-length jacket, and an expensive-looking watch. He had dark hair, cropped closely but not severely. Although no taller or heavier than average, he carried himself just like she remembered—with a coiled energy that seemed about to burst from the hiking boots on his feet. Rem's eyes locked on hers, and she stared into them against her better judgment. They looked like black bullets, only alive.

Her face warming, Jenna wondered again if Rem remembered her; they'd graduated high school together twelve years ago.

"Long time no see," he said.

7

She glanced down. "I'm surprised you remember me."

"How could I forget?" he said. "Yeah, you've changed a little, but I'd recognize those eyes anywhere. Bluest things since God made the sky. You're Jenna Newsome, former editor of the *Hilltop High Herald*. Best student in every English class ever taught at Hilltop, head of the Code of Conduct Council, and secretary of the Bible Club. A most serious young woman, if I recall correctly."

"You recall more than I'd like," she said, trying to ignore the flirty comment about her eyes.

"I saw you a few years ago at my mom's funeral," he said. "I asked my dad about you; he said you'd moved up to Winston-Salem for a while but then came home. What brought you back?"

"It's not worth telling," she said, firmly shaking her head. "It grieved me when your mama passed."

"It surprised me you attended her funeral," he said.

"She went to my church. I wanted to pay my respects."

"That's right." He laughed. "Everybody goes to everybody's funeral up here on the mountain."

"And they bring a casserole to the house beforehand."

A cell phone rang, and Rem held up a hand to put Jenna on hold, pulled a sleek little gadget from his pocket, and stepped back a few steps to take the call. Something in the gesture bothered Jenna, and she suddenly recalled that Rem had always annoyed her, that he seemed to treat people like they worked for him. Although no one else ever appeared to notice this, Jenna had long ago reached the conclusion that Rem Lincoln was a snob.

Part of her wanted to forgive him for the trait. After all, he'd moved to Hilltop at a hard time—the summer before his junior year, when his dad became the chief of the four-man police department. Another part, however, felt no pity whatsoever, because Rem had quickly taken the little town by storm. A star athlete, he'd played quarterback on the football team, point guard in basketball, and pitcher during baseball season. In addition to his abilities in anything competitive, he'd also whipped through his studies, particularly excelling in math. Cutting a wide swath in the eight-hundred-student school, he'd picked up friends as easily as a black skirt picks up lint and by his senior year had become class president and earned the "Most Likely to Succeed" superlative. Every girl in the school had fallen in love with him, Jenna included, and it seemed he'd eventually gotten around to dating all of them but her.

Rem closed his cell phone and moved back to her. "Sorry," he said. "A pressing situation."

"You were always busy," she said stiffly.

He pocketed the phone. "I've got to make a business decision," he explained. "Almost the end of the year; taxes and all."

"What are you doing home?" she asked, a slight edge rising unbidden in her voice. "Couldn't you do your business better in . . . well . . . where do you live now?"

"Atlanta. Yeah, guess you're right. But my dad, his heart isn't so good, and it's been a while since I saw him. Figured I'd come for Christmas this year, flew in a couple of hours ago."

He pulled a prescription slip from his jacket and held it up. "He sent me to pick up his medication."

"What's wrong with his heart?"

"The usual. High cholesterol, some clogging in the arteries—too much bacon and eggs, that kind of thing. He never exercises now that he's retired. Not that he did much before."

"He getting a bypass?"

"Not sure. Since Mama died, he doesn't seem interested in much of anything, his health included. I come through every now and again to check on him, usually for a day or so. He doesn't seem to care if I'm here or not."

Jenna thought of her parents. Although both were alive, they'd been divorced for about seven years and seemed to find most of their pleasure by making each other miserable. She usually got caught in the middle.

"I hope your dad gets better," she said.

Rem shrugged. "He's sixty-six. Getting older isn't for sissies."

Jenna smiled but only briefly.

"Age isn't bothering you," Rem said. "Unless it's for the better."

Jenna waved off his flippant charm, but her heart jumped a little just the same, and she remembered the first time she'd ever talked to Rem, the interview she'd done for the school paper. Serious about her writing, she'd wanted to give the students of her isolated hamlet a sense of what it felt like to transfer to a new place. Pen and pad in hand, she'd approached him after basketball practice near the middle of the season. For some odd reason, he'd seemed familiar as they sat down on the bleachers a few feet from the court. Although she knew it was crazy, she'd felt like she'd met him somewhere. She'd started to say something about the weird sensation, but her courage had failed as she opened her mouth, and she'd moved straight to the interview.

Surprisingly, Rem had revealed little about his background, only that his dad—a policeman in Knoxville— had gotten shot in a drug bust and a few months later loaded everybody up and moved them to Hilltop, where his family had long held some land.

"I had no choice in the move," Rem had told her matter-of-factly. "I'll make the most of it until graduation, then *sayonara*."

She'd pressed him to tell how it felt to leave old friends, what he liked about Hilltop, what he didn't, what was hard, what was easy. But he'd refused to discuss any of that.

"Don't ever look back," he'd said, his eyes distant and his tone slightly weary. "Something might be gaining on you."

Looking back now, the words sounded too mature for a seventeen-year-old and vaguely sad too, but she'd not understood that then and had left the interview frustrated and a little angry. Not only had she not gotten the story she wanted but Rem had made no romantic advances, and since he'd made a play on just about every other attractive girl in school, that had bothered her a lot. Wasn't she pretty enough for him?

Rem pointed to Mickey's picture. "A sick kid, huh?"

Jenna blinked back to the present and reminded herself she wasn't a teenager anymore. So what if Rem hadn't tried to charm her when they were high school classmates? She didn't like him anyway; his ways were too forward for a good Christian girl.

"Yeah, a sick kid," she said.

"What's wrong with him?"

"Myelodysplastic syndrome. We need money for a bone marrow transplant."

"A form of cancer, right?"

"How do you know that?"

"It's a long story," he offered. "How long you been here?"

She glanced at her watch and saw it was already 9:15. Her eyes suddenly felt grainy, and she wished she could take out her contacts, change into soft pajamas, and sip some hot tea.

"Since about six," she said. "Came right after work."

"How long you staying?"

"Store closes at ten. I'll pack up then."

"Makes for a long day, I guess."

She shrugged.

"Can I buy a cake?" he asked. "Help the kid out?"

"Sure," she said. "They're fifteen dollars."

Rem pulled out his wallet and handed her a hundred-dollar bill. She bagged the cake and gave it to him, then started counting out change.

"Keep it," he said.

"You sure?"

"Yeah, no problem. Tough break about the boy. How'd you get so involved?"

She almost asked him why he cared but held her tongue and put the hundred dollars in the cash box. "Mickey's family moved here last summer. I direct the day care he started attending. His father took a job as a custodian at the high school. But Mickey got sick before the family insurance kicked in."

"That's insane," Rem said.

She nodded. "I know. But we've done everything we can do. Hired a lawyer, talked to the insurance company until we're blue in the face. But everything's by the book, no exceptions."

"The boy's going to die if he doesn't get this transplant?"

"Yep."

Rem's face reddened, and a vein in his neck seemed ready to pop. His concern surprised Jenna, and she wondered why this mattered to him. He'd leave town the day after Christmas and never think of Mickey again.

A woman with a couple of children stepped up behind Rem, and Jenna decided to move Rem along.

"Good to see you," she said. "Take care of yourself."

He propped a hand on the table and gave her a slightly crooked grin, and Jenna's spine suddenly felt like someone had run a frozen feather up and down it. Where had she seen him before? Not high school, but somewhere else . . .

"I'm here through Christmas," Rem said softly. "Maybe we could get a cup of coffee in the next couple of days."

Jenna saw no reason to drink coffee with a man who

would disappear in a few days. "I don't like coffee," she said.

"Lunch then," he insisted. "You eat, don't you?"

Jenna glanced at the woman and children behind Rem. The children pulled at the woman's skirt, and she looked anxious to get going. Jenna looked back at Rem and thought she saw a touch of sadness in his eyes, perhaps even loneliness. Her heart softened, and she almost said yes but then remembered another man from about four years back, a man who had cut up her heart and left it in little clumps. She'd sworn she'd never let that happen again. Of all the men she needed to avoid, Rem Lincoln stood at the top of the list. To go out with him made absolutely no sense at all.

"I'm awfully busy between now and Christmas," she finally said.

"For old times' sake," he pressed. "There's not much of my old gang around anymore."

Jenna's bad feelings about Rem roiled back up. "I was never part of your old gang," she sniffed.

Rem threw out a hand, palm out in defeat. "Okay, tiger," he said. "I meant no offense."

"None taken," she said, slightly regretful of her attitude.

Rem picked up his cake. "Can't blame a man for trying," he said.

Jenna nodded. "Merry Christmas."

"Take care."

Rem walked away, and Jenna gave her attention to the woman and children. The woman's jeans were old and the children's shoes scuffed and worn.

"Cakes are fifteen," Jenna said. "Pies are ten. All the money goes to the Mickey's Miracle Fund."

The woman opened her wallet, and Jenna saw she didn't have much money. "Make it five for either," she said. "The cakes aren't as fresh as they were this morning."

The woman smiled and handed her ten dollars, and Jenna gave her a cake and a pie. The woman and children moved off, and Jenna pulled fifteen dollars from her purse, added it to the ten from the woman, and put it in the cash box. The store fell quiet for a second, and she glanced around and saw Rem in the pharmacy at the edge of the store. He had his cell phone to his ear as he waited for his prescription, and she wondered what kind of work he did that stayed busy right up to Christmas. Important stuff, she guessed; he dressed like he had money.

She glanced down at her clothes—a pullover wool sweater that matched her eyes and a pair of black slacks that fit well against her slender but well-toned legs. She touched her earrings, a pair of simple aquamarine studs. Although nearly thirty, she kept in shape by lifting a few weights about three times a week and running on the treadmill in her mother's basement. She'd blossomed since high school; everybody said so. Lost all her baby fat, let her hair grow some, wore contacts now instead of glasses. A lot of men found her attractive, and she knew if she lived in a bigger town, she'd receive a lot of male attention. Of course, she'd tried that once, and it hadn't worked out too well.

She sighed as her mood dropped. Here she was, a month shy of her thirtieth birthday, and the sight of an acquaintance from high school caused her this much nostalgia. What was wrong? Rem made her heart race. So what? His kind and hers didn't match. Even if he suddenly announced he planned to settle in Hilltop and wanted to start seeing her, she wouldn't go out with him. His type brought trouble; she knew that from her past. A woman of faith didn't waste time with men like Rem Lincoln. She'd decided that a long time ago and saw no reason to change it now.

Rem pocketed his cell phone, and Jenna turned back to her pies and cakes. An elderly woman stepped to the table and Jenna said hello, but her mind stayed on Rem. Why did he disturb her so? Why did he feel so familiar? What if he called her and asked her out? She'd say no, that's what. She did hope he called though. At least then she'd get the satisfaction of having been asked.

2

His dad's prescription in his jacket pocket, Rem hopped into his silver Lexus LX 470 with the bike rack on top and headed down the main street of Hilltop. A black dog with gray on his face sat on the seat beside him. Christmas lights draped the street, and Rem leaned back and opened a window. Cold burned into his face, but he didn't care. He patted the dog and gazed out at the small town. Sitting about thirty miles northwest of Asheville, Hilltop boasted three main roads, a couple of nearby ski resorts, and a waterfall a mile from the central square that people swore they could hear from the front steps of the city hall on quiet summer nights. Barely three thousand people lived in Hilltop. Rem turned left and headed toward his old school.

"It's not the same without Mom," he said sadly to the dog.

The dog snuffled as if in agreement.

The air felt like snow, and Rem hoped a few inches would fall. Maybe that would make him feel more

17

cheerful. He patted the dog again. "Maybe I shouldn't have come home, Boomer. What you think?"

Boomer licked his hand. The lights of the Lexus lit up the school, and Rem slowed as he passed it. Memories flooded back. Without planning it, he suddenly turned the Lexus into the parking lot and wheeled toward the back of the main building. Near the gym he parked, threw open the door, and stepped down. Boomer climbed out behind him. The dim outlines of the school's athletic fields lay straight ahead. Although quiet now, those fields had once served as his home, the place where he let loose every ounce of energy he possessed, every tension he ever felt, every bolt of anger he ever experienced. He'd ruled on those fields and in the gym just above them, had bent games to his will. Maybe that's why he'd loved athletics so much. Given his natural talents and iron nerves, he could control what happened there, could maneuver life to fit his desires, could steer it away from the whim of random chance.

"Can't do that anywhere else," he said to Boomer. "No matter how hard you try." Boomer licked his lips as if in agreement.

Rem studied the school's dark outline. He'd moved to Hilltop kicking and screaming, his young life a shambles. If he'd had his way, he and his folks never would have left Knoxville, the opportunities that city offered him, the friends he'd known since birth. But hey, sometimes you don't get what you want. Sometimes life kicks you in the teeth, and you have to pick yourself up from the floor, wipe the blood from your mouth, and move on. Otherwise you might as well just curl up, whimper a little, and die. But that was one thing Rem didn't do; no whimpering from him, no sir, no how.

Driven by that attitude, he'd made the most of his two years in Hilltop, turned a pig's hide into a silk suit, earned a baseball scholarship to North Carolina State. After that he'd hustled away from the little hamlet as fast as he could. Since then he'd returned only as often as necessary to see his folks.

Now he was back in town to see his sick father and deal with a whole lot of worries he'd just as soon not have to face. "What you think I should do, Boomer?" he asked.

Boomer raised his head but didn't offer any advice.

"That's what I figured," Rem said. "You're as clueless as I am."

Jenna's face reared up in Rem's head, and he smiled ruefully and scratched Boomer behind the ears. "I saw an old friend," Rem said. "But she didn't seem too glad to see me."

Boomer tilted his head to hear more, but Rem thought better of it, lifted the dog into the Lexus, climbed back in, and headed home. In less than ten minutes, he'd parked in front of his dad's two-story white house and gone inside, Boomer slow but steady at his heels. After hanging his jacket on a hat tree in the foyer, Rem clomped across the hardwood floors to the front room, where he found his dad in a rocking chair, an almost-dead fire struggling to stay lit in a stone hearth to his right. No decorations marked the room, nothing to show that Christmas was only four days away. A big-screen television played a basketball game, and his dad barely looked up as he entered.

"Who's winning?" Rem asked.

"Carolina. By four."

Rem pulled out the medicine he'd picked up and sat it on the table. "You eat anything yet?" he asked.

"A bowl of soup. That Progresso's pretty good if you sprinkle some cheese on it."

Rem grunted. His dad paid no attention to what he ate. If you spread cheese on a roof tile, he'd probably swallow it, no questions asked. No wonder his heart was in bad shape. Rem threw a couple of logs on the fire and poked at the embers to get the blaze going. After a couple of minutes, he felt satisfied with the work and sagged into the chair by his dad's rocker and inspected him. Roscoe Lincoln. Former semipro baseball player with a host of North Carolina and Tennessee barnstorming teams. After he got too old for that, he married his sweetheart, Eva, settled down, and became a policeman in Knoxville. For a long time Roscoe had kept his athlete's physique, jogging regularly and doing push-ups and sit-ups at night as he watched a game on television. But then . . . well, the year before they moved to Hilltop, a man had put a bullet in his thigh and all that had changed. His waistline had ballooned like somebody had puffed it up with an air machine, and he'd rounded out into a barrel-bellied, cigarette-smoking poster child for heart disease. Not a pretty picture, and it had only gotten worse since Eva had died. Although Rem had tried at least a thousand times to talk his dad into better habits, it did about as much good as asking a fourteen-year-old boy to listen to classical music.

"You take your medicine like you should?" Rem asked.

20

Roscoe grunted and hit the television clicker. The channel flipped to a news report. Somebody had shot three people in Atlanta, a "holiday massacre," said the reporter.

Rem tried something else. "You want to go shopping tomorrow? Get a tree maybe? A few lights to hang up?"

"What for? Not much to celebrate, the way I see it."

Boomer moved to Rem's feet and lay down. "You going back to the doctor after Christmas?" Rem asked.

"I guess." Roscoe flipped the controls back to the basketball game.

"I'll come home if you have surgery or anything."

Roscoe nodded but didn't look at him. "You're a good son," he said. "But you don't need to do that."

"I know. You can take care of yourself."

"That's right."

Rem watched the basketball game a few minutes. Never a man for a lot of chatter, his dad had gotten even quieter since his mom's death, and the constant effort to talk, to find something in common with his dad, wore Rem out when he came home. Even watching sports had become an ordeal. Ever since . . . well . . . He pushed away the bad memory. His dad didn't mind watching games with him now, but talking about the contests seemed beyond his capability. For all Roscoe seemed to care, he and Rem could watch a thousand games a day but never say a word about anything that truly mattered.

Frustrated, Rem stood and threw more wood on the

fire. He hated coming home, hated the way it made him feel, the loneliness it put in his gut, the way it made him feel cut off from everything, his mom, his dad, his . . .

He moved back to his chair and tried conversation once more, this time choosing a new track, hoping it would pique his dad's interest at least enough to get a few words from him. "You know anything new about Jenna Newsome?" he asked.

Roscoe looked up, his eyes confused, but didn't speak for a second.

"Jenna Newsome," Rem repeated. "What's the latest scoop on her?"

"Why do you ask?" Roscoe asked, momentarily attentive.

"I saw her earlier tonight."

Roscoe grunted. "She's an attractive woman, I know that." He studied the basketball game again. North Carolina had fallen behind by three with less than two minutes to go.

"I saw her at the grocery," Rem said. "She's trying to raise money for some kid's medical costs."

"That's right," Roscoe said, his attention never leaving the screen. "I read about it in the paper. She's a do-gooder. Least that's what your mama always said."

"What brought her back to Hilltop from Winston-Salem?"

The game went to a commercial. Roscoe turned to Rem. "Why this sudden interest in Jenna Newsome? Not enough women in Atlanta to keep you busy?"

"Don't you worry about that. Just tell me about Jenna."

"Okay, okay," Roscoe said. "I don't know details; don't listen to a lot of gossiping."

"Just tell me what you know," Rem insisted.

Roscoe muted the television and actually focused on Rem for a change. "You got something for this woman?" he asked.

"Heavens no. I just thought I'd ask her out, catch up on local news. A cup of coffee with an attractive woman might actually make this trip worthwhile. You're not exactly a party on a stick, you know."

Roscoe chuckled. "If it'll keep you gone so I can watch my games in peace, I'm all for it."

"So what's the story with her?"

"You promise you'll go out with her?"

"I promise I'll ask."

Roscoe nodded. "Your mama, rest her soul, said something once about Jenna getting jilted at the altar. Some real estate man in Winston-Salem left her high and dry right before their wedding. She went to school at Wake Forest, used to be owned by the Baptists, I think."

"She never married?"

"Not according to your mama, and she went to church with her. Your mama said she heard that Jenna was teaching school there—second graders, I think—when she met this man. Dated him close to four years before he high-tailed it out right before walking the aisle."

"That's got to be rough."

"No doubt about that."

"Why'd the guy wig out on her?"

"Who knows? Guys these days get crazy when it comes to marriages—you know that. Here you are thirty and no closer to a wedding altar than a pig to a bath. Am I right?"

Rem nodded. Boomer stood and looked at him. He scratched the old dog behind the ears. "She seeing anybody now?"

Roscoe eyed him scornfully. "What do I look like, the editor of the society column?"

"Just asking."

The game came back on, and Rem knew better than to interrupt the last couple of minutes. Maryland made a shot, then Carolina. Rem thought of Jenna, figured how hurt she must have been when her fiancé bolted, how ashamed she must have felt moving back to Hilltop. *What kind of man would do that to a woman?* he wondered. *Date her for years then disappear when the moment of truth arrived.*

Half-watching the game, he quickly surveyed his own love life. Although he'd dated enough women to fill a baseball stadium, he'd only gotten serious with a couple of them, and he'd never given even one a ring. Yeah, he'd dumped a few pretty hard with little or no explanation, but he'd never treated a woman as poorly as this man had treated Jenna.

North Carolina's point guard made a last-second shot, and the crowd went crazy with celebration. Roscoe flipped the television back to the news, and Rem felt it safe to repeat his question. "Is she dating anybody?"

Roscoe punched the mute button again and gave Rem his full attention. "What's got into you?" he asked. "You see a girl you barely know, and all of a sudden you're the FBI, asking so many questions. And don't give me the shovelful that you're just looking for a little company so you won't have to hang out with me."

Rem scratched his chin and tried to figure it out. Truth was, it didn't make much sense. "I knew her in high school," he offered.

"I don't recall you ever asked her out."

"True."

"Why not?"

"I don't know. She was pretty enough, but sort of shy, more than I liked at the time, almost bookish."

"She's a bit straight with her religion too; least that's what I've heard. She like that in school?"

"Yeah, always gave off this 'pure as the driven snow' air. Not that I was a wild man or anything, but Jenna carried a reputation as a straight-laced girl."

"You wanted a little more action, that it?"

"Maybe."

"So what's the attraction now? I don't think she's changed."

Rem eyed his dad and tried to figure it out. Was it plain old loneliness? Nostalgia for a youth he no longer possessed? The need to talk to somebody about his difficulties?

Rem hung his head and decided not to lie, at least not to himself. He knew why Jenna attracted him. The same reason he'd stayed away from her in high school, and it had little or nothing to do with her religious scruples. Those blue eyes—he'd seen them years before high school, the year he'd turned eight . . .

Rem blinked and pushed away the memory and focused on his dad again, his feelings confused.

"I'm home for Christmas," Rem said. "Got some

things going on, business stuff, you know how it can get. I need somebody to talk to, and you . . . well . . ."

He stopped and let the sentence trail away. His dad knew the nature of their relationship. No reason to spell it out. Although he didn't have a clue that Jenna would or should become a friend, he wanted somebody to talk to this year, somebody to share a laugh with, somebody to make him feel warm and alive.

Roscoe dropped his head, and Rem saw that he understood it too, the separation between them—the distance as wide as a gorge between two mountaintops. Was it inevitable that life brought a father and son to this point? Carried them to separate islands where they both stood all alone no matter how hard they tried to escape?

"What else you want to know about her?" Roscoe asked, breaking the awkward silence.

Rem sat up a little straighter. "Anything you can tell me."

"She lives in an apartment," Roscoe said as if reciting a phone book. "Goes by her mama's house most every day. Margaret is a pill; you might know that already. As demanding as a staff sergeant at boot camp. I saw her at the doctor's office a few months ago. They didn't get her in right at her appointment time. She raised more stink than a skunk at a church picnic. She'll hardly let Jenna out of her sight. From what I hear, the old woman's bitter about her husband divorcing her. Fusses about him every chance she gets to whoever will listen."

"How long they been divorced?"

"Six, seven years, I guess. A couple of years before

Jenna moved back. Surprised you hadn't heard about it."

"I think I did but only vaguely. Not home much in those days, you'll recall."

"Not here much in these days either."

"You want me around more?"

"I can take care of myself."

Rem let the matter drop and moved back to Jenna. "She said she directed a day care."

"Yeah, the Kid's Delight Day Care. I think it's part of a chain that operates a number of for-profit centers in small towns in North Carolina. Must have a pretty good head on her shoulders to make one of those things go. They got close to a hundred kids, I think."

"She must like children."

"Guess so."

Rem looked away as old memories flooded back. His eyes watered, but he wiped them quickly and ground his teeth to cut off the flow. He got sentimental like this every Christmas no matter what he did to prevent it.

Uncomfortable with the emotional boil in his stomach, he stood, moved to the fireplace, and stared at a twenty-two-year-old picture of his family, the joyous look on everyone's face, a look he'd not seen in a long time. He picked up the picture and faced his dad again. "You ever think about back then?" he asked, pointing at the picture.

Roscoe glanced at him but didn't speak.

Rem studied the picture a few more seconds, then set it back on the mantel. "I wish we could talk about it," he said.

"Talking changes nothing," Roscoe said.

27

"You can't tell me you don't think about it. I know you do."

Roscoe stared at him, a touch of anger in his eyes. "I think about it every day," he said. "But you know the rule. We don't talk about what we can't fix. And we can't fix this. Couldn't then, couldn't now."

Rem moved to Boomer and squatted next to his old friend. "Will you listen to me?" he asked the dog.

Boomer panted and showed his teeth in a sad smile. "Sure," he seemed to say, "I'll listen. Haven't I always?"

Rem looked back at his dad. "Christmas is rough."

Roscoe fingered the television controls. The sound of the news announcer once more filled the room, and Rem knew the conversation had ended. He stood and pulled out his cell phone. "I'll be in my room," he told Roscoe.

Roscoe nodded but didn't look up. With Boomer at his heels, Rem stepped to his dad, touched him on the shoulder, and headed to his room. Like every Christmas since that one twenty-two years ago, he'd once again spend the holidays pretty much alone.

❦3❦

After the grocery store closed, Jenna packed up the desserts she hadn't sold, put them in the trunk of her car, and drove immediately to Mickey Strack's house, a square, boxlike, wood-framed place about two miles outside Hilltop. Brenda Strack met her at the door, her brown hair tied in a ponytail, her feet bare on the wood floor, her skinny body dressed in worn jeans and a Carolina Panthers sweatshirt. Jenna handed Brenda an apple pie as she entered. Brenda pointed her to the seat she always took on the sofa when she visited, then brought the pie to the kitchen.

Suddenly weary from the long day, Jenna took a breath and glanced around the room. A blue sofa, a lamp on a table on the right, no table on the left. Two chairs, one an easy chair that matched the sofa, the other a wood piece with a slatted back. A fireplace, but no fire burned in it. Not much decorated the walls. Although not poor, the Stracks didn't own much, and Mickey's medical bills guaranteed that probably wouldn't change.

Brenda stepped back into the room, perched on the

arm of the easy chair across from Jenna, and smiled warmly. Jenna marveled at her attitude. Although not blessed with much education or refinement, Brenda displayed a natural graciousness not many possessed. In spite of all her troubles, she kept her head about her and seemed greatly appreciative of what others had tried to do for her and her family.

"Tess in bed?" Jenna asked.

"About thirty minutes ago."

"She's a brave girl," Jenna said.

"She wants to help her brother," Brenda said. "She's not sure what everything means, but she knows Mickey is sick and her blood can help him."

Jenna nodded. If they could raise the money for the transplant, Tess's little body would provide the bone marrow for the procedure. Mickey would go into an isolation unit in the hospital at Duke University. The doctors would give him chemotherapy first, then radiation treatments. The chemo and radiation would reduce Mickey's immune system to zero, putting him in danger of dying even as they prepared him for his only chance to live. If he lived through those treatments, they'd then transplant Tess's stem cells into his body. If all went well, his body would accept her cells and they'd regenerate and create a new breed of compatible blood, a new immune system, and a healthy baby boy. The whole process would take at least two months, and Mickey would live in a sterile room without direct human contact the whole time. At best, he had less than a 50 percent chance of survival.

"How's Mickey today?" Jenna asked.

"Weaker," Brenda said. "His color is bad. I'm going

back to the hospital in a few minutes. Tom's with him now."

Jenna nodded. She knew the routine from her frequent visits over the last two months. Tom worked at the school all day while Brenda—who had quit her job as a waitress when they'd discovered Mickey's illness—stayed with the baby. When Tom got off, he took the watch at the hospital while Brenda spent time with Tess. Since they'd learned of Mickey's sickness, they'd spent little time as a couple and almost none all together with Tess.

"We're making progress," Jenna said, trying to lift Brenda's spirits. "Got in a couple of checks today, sold some pies at Turley's Grocery. Have over forty thousand dollars now."

Brenda sighed, and Jenna shared her sadness in spite of her efforts at cheerfulness. Forty thousand left them a long way short. Unless something changed, Mickey wouldn't make it more than a few more weeks. Everybody knew it, even the most optimistic of those who'd tried to make this miracle happen.

A sense of failure rolled through Jenna, and she thought back to the events that had led to this point.

The Strack family had lived in Greensboro before moving to Hilltop in mid-June on the advice of an aunt who'd told Tom about the job at the school. Since his work with the school didn't start until mid-August, Tom had taken a short-term position on the grounds crew of a golf course about five miles away, and Brenda had started as a waitress at Hilltop's favorite diner, Bud's Barbecue. That's when Mickey showed up at Jenna's day care.

"Aunt Martha can handle our six-year-old when she's not in school," Brenda told Jenna the day she brought Mickey by. "But she says she's not up to handling a baby anymore."

Jenna fell in love with Mickey the first time she saw him. Who wouldn't? He grabbed her nose as she bent to hold him, his big brown eyes staring into hers like he knew her name. He smiled when she spoke to him, and two dimples as cute as any on a movie screen graced his chubby cheeks.

From the end of June to the first of August, Jenna met Brenda almost every morning as she delivered Mickey, and the cherubic boy quickly became her favorite baby. Perhaps it was because she liked Brenda and Tom so much. Or maybe it was because Mickey was the youngest child she had in the day care. Or maybe it was because she'd always figured to have a baby about his age of her own by now. At least that's the way she'd always seen it unfolding. Get married at about twenty-five or so, spend three or four years getting to know her husband, give birth sometime before her thirtieth birthday. Mickey could have been her boy if her marriage plans hadn't fallen apart when she least expected it. Why shouldn't she love him like the baby boy she'd never had?

Mickey's first symptoms showed up the first day of August. A high fever, congested cough, labored breathing. Brenda and Tom waited only a day to see if he'd get better, and when he didn't they made an appointment with Dr. Will Russell, the town's young pediatrician. Dr. Russell put Mickey on antibiotics and ordered some tests. At first the baby responded to the medicine and all seemed well. But then, less than two weeks later, he came down with another fever and even worse congestion. Dr. Russell diagnosed pneumonia and ordered more testing.

It surprised them all when the bills for the tests started coming back with notations that they had no insurance to pay for them. That was one of the reasons Tom had wanted the school job in the first place—the state provided good benefits.

"Your insurance began once you started work," the school administrator told Tom when he visited his office. "You brought Mickey to the doctor four days before that."

"But my boy was already sick," Tom said. "You expect me to wait till I start work to take him to a doctor?"

The administrator, a kind man who obviously wanted to help, made a couple of phone calls to the authorities in Asheville, but his efforts proved fruitless. "No exceptions," he reported to Tom. "Policies have to be followed." Although furious, Tom shook his head, thanked the administrator, and left his office.

The really bad news started coming in a few days later. Mickey's platelet count, the clotting cells in his blood, numbered only sixty thousand, with normal levels at close to two hundred to three hundred thousand. Also, his white cell count—the cells that fight disease—were over four times higher than the normal of seven to ten thousand. It took almost a month to get all the test results back. Dr. Russell called Tom and Brenda into his office.

"Mickey's real sick," he said plainly.

"What do you mean?" Tom asked.

"Let me put it in layman's terms," Dr. Russell said.

"Mickey's got a blood condition that destroys his immune system. Diseases that most people never catch grab onto him like a dog on a bone. To have any chance at all, Mickey's got to have a bone marrow transplant."

Tom and Brenda sat openmouthed with shock.

"They can do it in Durham," Dr. Russell continued. "I've already talked to some folks there. They'd like to see him as soon as possible."

Tom found his voice. "It can't be," he said. "Why should something like this happen to us? What's Mickey done to deserve it? He's just a baby."

Dr. Russell shrugged. "I'm not a preacher," he said.

"What'll all this cost?" Brenda asked.

"Close to two hundred fifty thousand," Dr. Russell said. "Your insurance will cover it."

Brenda shook her head. "There's a problem with that. We're trying to get it cleared up."

"What's the deal?" Dr. Russell asked.

"They're saying our insurance didn't start until Tom's first day at the school. We brought Mickey in a few days before that."

"I'm sure it's some fouled-up paperwork, that's all."

"Hope so," Tom said. "Otherwise we can't pay you, the hospital either. Two hundred fifty thousand might as well be ten million."

"Let me do some calling," Dr. Russell said. "Maybe I can find some doctors who will work with you at a reduced rate."

"But that won't pay the hospital," Brenda said.

"No," Dr. Russell said. "It won't. Check your insurance again. I'll call Asheville for you."

Tom and Brenda thanked him and left his office. Later

that night, Brenda told Jenna of the visit with Dr. Russell and the staggering cost of the transplant.

"He says it's Mickey's only chance," Brenda said, her eyes puffy from tears. "But if the insurance doesn't pay, we have no way to come up with that money."

To Tom and Brenda's relief, Dr. Russell continued to treat Mickey in spite of their inability to pay him, and the administrator at the Hilltop hospital said he wouldn't refuse treatments to a baby either, no matter how poor the family.

The telephone rang, jolting Jenna back to the present. Brenda picked up the phone and left the room. Jenna stood and moved to one of the two square windows on the front of the house. Outside, the wind moved the bare branches of a large maple that fronted the house. Jenna shivered and again thought of the last few months.

Guided by Dr. Russell, Tom and Brenda had gotten in touch with Duke University Hospital, the nearest facility with the expertise to care for Mickey. Almost miraculously, testing showed that Tess's blood antigens matched Mickey's. Everyone rejoiced that the one-in-four chance of finding a sibling match had come through in Mickey's only sibling. That had taken another month. Mickey's health bounced up and down, sick one week, healthy the next.

The doctors at Duke scheduled the transplant for the second week in January, then sent Mickey and his family back to Hilltop. Tom appealed to the state for coverage of Mickey's condition, and the local school board supported his action. Unfortunately, the authorities in Raleigh refused to change the decision in Asheville.

"A preexisting illness," said the state report. "No exceptions to the policy."

The first snow fell the first week of November, and Mickey's white blood count, so steady for several weeks, worsened. He lay listless in his crib at the hospital.

For a couple of days, everybody walked around in a daze, not sure what to do next. Jenna went to see Tom and Brenda every day, her heart breaking for the young family. "We have to do something," she kept saying. "We can't just give up."

"But what?" they always asked. "Our hospital can't do this, and Duke won't do it without somebody paying for it."

Although not sure what she expected or even wanted from him, Jenna took the matter to her pastor before the week ended. Rev. Nelson Hart, a square-jawed fullback of a man no more than a few years older than her, listened intently as she spoke, his eyes bright, his thick body tense.

"Tom and Brenda are good folks," he said after Jenna finished describing the situation. "I visited them a couple of times after they moved here."

"I never saw them in church."

"No, they never took me up on my invitations but didn't seem opposed to it either. If Mickey hadn't turned up sick, I expect they'd have come sooner or later."

Jenna nodded. Brenda had seemed fairly interested when she'd invited her to church. But then Mickey became ill, and everything in Brenda's life flipped upside down. Of course, Mickey's condition gave Brenda and Tom even more need of a church family.

"We've had them on the prayer list," Nelson

said. "Maybe we should have a healing service for them."

Jenna nodded but wasn't satisfied. At this point not even a healing service seemed like enough. An idea came to her, and she opened her mouth to speak but then hesitated. Although a native of Hilltop, Nelson had become pastor of Hilltop Community barely two years ago, and a lot of people weren't sure about him yet, weren't comfortable with some of the changes he'd suggested since he replaced the aged, well-trusted Rev. Hamrick. Although Jenna liked most of what he'd done and found his wife, Julie, a delight, she knew that others weren't so pleased with his leadership style, his willingness to try new things. He hardly ever wore a tie during the week, jogged through town almost every afternoon in basketball shorts, and sometimes preached from a Bible translation that wasn't the King James Version. The first seminary-trained pastor in the history of the church, he didn't shout as much as Rev. Hamrick had, and a few of the old-timers saw him as too smart for his own good, maybe theirs as well.

Not wanting to get Nelson in any trouble, Jenna closed her mouth.

"What?" Nelson asked, leaning closer. "What did you want to say?"

"Nothing," Jenna said. "Don't want to stir anything up."

Nelson folded his arms across his chest. Jenna admired his easy way. He'd gone to Hilltop High a few years before her, then went off for his education and early ministry training. She wondered why he'd decided to come back. If she ever again got a chance to get out, she'd take it and never look back. Maybe someday . . .

"I'm good at stirring up," the reverend said. "Or haven't you heard?"

"I've heard."

"So tell me what's on your mind."

"Okay, I've got an idea," Jenna said. "But I'm not sure the church can help."

Nelson placed his hands on his desk. "Try me," he said.

Jenna raised an eyebrow. "What if we raise the money for Mickey Strack's treatment?" she offered. "Make it a church project."

Nelson's eyes narrowed, and she thought she'd lost him.

"I know it's unusual," she quickly added. "But Mickey's situation is unusual. What more loving thing could we do than to care for a child? Instead of sending our Christmas offering overseas this year, we could make this our Christmas mission."

"We usually collect about ten thousand dollars," the reverend said. "That's a long way from what you need."

Jenna nodded. About a hundred and fifty people a week attended their church. No way could they come up with all the money. She broadened her idea. "What if we invite everybody in town to help?" she asked. "The other churches, Baptist, Methodist, Catholic, all of them."

"We don't usually do much with the mainline churches," Nelson said. "Not sure our crowd will go for that."

"I know," Jenna agreed.

Nelson stood and looked out his window. "I'm not against this," he said. "I want you to know that. But it'll take some study, some prayer. Give me a couple of days to study it."

She agreed to do that, and less than a week later Nelson called her and told her he'd do what he could. They'd need to make it a community effort, he said. He'd already talked to some folks at the bank. They could set up an account there and invite anyone who wanted to make a donation. An accountant from the Methodist church had agreed to handle the fund to give people confidence the money would be properly managed.

"I've talked to some elders too," he told her. "I think we can get our Christmas mission money to go toward this, at least half of it."

Now, just over forty thousand dollars later, here she sat, right before Christmas and a long way from their goal. Brenda appeared back in the room, the phone in her hand. Jenna pushed back her hair.

"That was the bank," Brenda said. "We got three pretty good checks today. Up to forty-eight thousand dollars."

Jenna smiled, but her energy suddenly ebbed to almost nothing. Although she didn't want to give up, they'd been at this since the second week of November, and in spite of great effort from hundreds of people, they were nowhere near their goal. If, as Dr. Russell had indicated more than once in the last few days, Mickey had less than a couple of months to live without the transplant, their time was fast running out.

"That's good," Jenna said. "We're making progress."

Brenda moved to her. "It's all because of you," she said.

"We've got a long way to go," Jenna cautioned.

"We can make it though, can't we?" Her eyes looked hopeful and yet afraid at the same time, and Jenna knew the young woman had come to depend heavily on her. How could she tell her what she really felt? That she didn't trust that they'd make it. That she feared she'd fail like she had so many times before, like with her parents when they were going through their hard times, how she couldn't hold them together in spite of her best efforts. Then later, Carl, the man she figured she'd marry. She'd come up empty there too. But how could she say any of that to Brenda?

"My church will give five thousand or so," she said, pushing down her distress. "That'll put us over fifty."

"You've told me to have faith," Brenda said. "I'm doing that. I'm having faith."

Jenna stood and took Brenda's hands in hers. She felt so old all of a sudden, like a woman with more miles on her body than she deserved. She wanted to speak the truth to Brenda and tell her that unless a true miracle happened, they had no more chance than a possum in the middle of the racetrack at the Charlotte 600. But how could she do that and destroy what little hope Brenda had left?

"We'll all have faith," she finally said. "That's what it's going to take."

Brenda smiled, and Jenna hugged her and told her she'd see her the next day. Then she left the house, her body weary and her soul discouraged. After climbing into her car, she leaned back and tried to pray but got

40

no spark for it. Right now her faith felt as tattered as a worn-out dishrag, and she didn't know how to mend it. All this effort had accomplished nothing. She felt so helpless, so useless, so guilty. Add up everything in her life, and what did you get? One big flop of a person. Yet she'd pretended to Brenda that they could still make it. Not only had she failed to raise the money they needed, but she'd also misled a distraught mom. What kind of person did that kind of thing?

She thought of Mickey and wanted to cry. Without a bolt-from-the-blue miracle, Mickey Strack would almost surely die, and since Jenna didn't really expect to see one of those, she felt absolutely helpless to stop his dying.

❧ 4 ❧

The snow that had threatened the night before failed to fall, and by ten o'clock the next day a bright sun had peeked out instead, its face strong in spite of the cold in the air. After a quick bite of brunch—two eggs, three pancakes, and some bacon his dad fried—Rem made a couple of short phone calls, then changed into his bike clothes for a ride.

"You going out like that?" Roscoe asked, pointing to the skin-tight pants and shirt Rem wore as he stepped back into the kitchen before leaving.

"Sure, I'm ripped and proud of it."

"Real men don't wear spandex."

Rem slipped on his helmet and gloves. "I won't tell anybody I'm kin to you," he said.

"Thank the Lord for small favors."

"I'm proud of you too, Pops."

"Maybe we can go get that tree you wanted when you get back."

Rem looked at his dad but decided not to make too

43

much of the suggestion lest he scare him off it. "That'll be good," he said.

Roscoe put a plate in the dishwasher, and Rem headed to his bike.

Five minutes later, he steered out of Hilltop and headed up the incline past the last gas station. The brisk air quickly reddened his face and got his blood pumping. The muscles in his legs pulsed with the pedaling of the bike, and he took a big breath of fresh air and looked up. The blue sky spilled down. The side of Hilltop Mountain bordered the road to his right; the sheer drop-off to the valley below stretched out to his left.

Rem smiled and adjusted his sunglasses. He loved riding his bike, especially in the mountains, loved the strain of the pedals going uphill, the sheer abandonment of flying down on the other side. When he rode, his problems somehow seemed smaller, almost as if each turn of the wheels put the troubles farther and farther in the rearview mirror. He needed that today, maybe more than ever.

The road eased gradually up the incline, then turned left about a mile out of town and wound like a snake around the side of the mountain. The wind kicked up from behind, and Rem appreciated the tailwind. Going up a mountain and into a wind would've made the ride more of a fight than he wanted today. About two miles out, the road switched back and became steeper. In spite of the cold, he began to perspire, and it felt good, cleansing. Close to thirty minutes passed. The road dropped off, and Rem began a rapid whip down the mountain. His spirits soared as his speed increased. The sun warmed his back. No matter how heavy his problems became, he could handle them; hadn't he always? He checked his speedometer—forty-four miles an hour!

Jenna's face popped into his head as he sped down the steep grade, and he smiled again. He'd call her when he got back home. Even though she'd said no last night, he'd convince her today, no doubt about it. Women always said yes to him; he could count on that no matter what else didn't work out. Yes sir, just as soon as he made it back home, he'd give Jenna another chance!

Rem wheeled to the bottom of the grade and eased back on his seat. The three miles down the hill had lasted only a few minutes. Now the road leveled out for a stretch of almost four miles. He saw a white fence to his left and then an arched entry down a gravel path. Suddenly realizing where he was, he slowed in respect and eased past the archway. About a quarter of a mile later, he came to a second gravel road, this one only one lane and bordered with thick brush. Making a quick decision, he turned left and pedaled down the one-lane road and into the cemetery. His pace slowed even more as he fought the gravel under his wheels. After a couple hundred yards, the gravel became soggy mud, and he eased off his bike and pushed it down the road. A rutted path appeared to his right, and he took it. Soon the path pretty much ended, and Rem lay down his bike and walked forward about seventy yards. Cedar trees bordered the white fence that lay straight ahead. Rem's breath quickened. He reached the spot not far from the fence, a flat grave in the middle of at least twenty others. A white stone stood at the grave's head.

Rem stopped, took off his bike helmet and sunglasses, and held them under his arm. In the distance he heard cars approaching but didn't look up. The sun felt cooler now even though no trees shaded him. He stared at the white stone, read the words written on it. "Eva Lincoln. 1942–2000. Wife. Mother. Woman of the Word."

His eyes misting like they always did when he visited his mom's grave, Rem squatted to the headstone and leaned in close. "I miss you," he whispered, ignoring the foolish feeling that hit him every time he did this. "Dad does too, though he might not say it to me."

A light breeze blew through Rem's hair, and a dog barked behind him. He patted the stone. "Merry Christmas," he said. "You know I love you."

The stone felt cold under his hand. He glanced around the graveyard, scanning the headstones nearest him, and his spirit sagged. Death came without warning most of the time, a sudden stab of hurt that twisted a life into rubble as surely as a tornado, a whirling black funnel that sucked up everything and left nothing untouched.

His mother had accepted her death with an ease that surprised him. Heart disease got her—a "bad ticker," she called it. Nothing short of a transplant could have provided any hope of saving her, and she saw no need of that.

"The Lord's got my time appointed," she'd told him and Roscoe the day the doctor told them that the left side of her heart had deteriorated to the point of no return. "If it's my hour, so be it."

Rem stayed angry at her for a long time after she said that. What kind of person didn't fight like a cornered rat, didn't claw and cling to life like superglue to duct tape? He didn't like it that his mom had embraced her end so gently and peacefully. Didn't she want to stay with him and his dad? He needed her. Roscoe did too.

"I got my reasons," she said when he pressed her to consider more drastic medical treatments.

"I know," he said. "But they're not good enough."

"They are for me."

Although Rem tried to get his dad to talk her into changing her mind, he couldn't do it. The discussion ended, and he never again brought it up.

Rem heard cars approaching and stood and slipped his helmet back on. The dog barked again, and Rem put on his sunglasses and decided to head out. Back on his bike, he saw the cars as they turned in at the cemetery's main gate—looked like ten or so. He wondered who had died. The cars headed his way, and he braked respectfully and waited for them to stop. A couple of minutes later, the lead car reached a spot a few feet from a green funeral cover and pulled over. The rest followed. A minute later the door of the lead car opened, and a man climbed out on the passenger side.

Rem almost fell off his bike as he recognized Nelson Hart. What was he doing in Hilltop?

Nelson moved to the hearse that had stopped behind him and took a spot at the back. Within a couple of minutes, the pallbearers unloaded a casket, hauled it ahead of the crowd to the funeral tent, and lay it across the dug-out grave. Nelson stepped to the head of the casket, opened his Bible, and began to read. His strong voice echoed across the quiet of the morning air.

Rem almost laughed. Nelson was a preacher? He couldn't believe it! Back when he'd known him, the gang called him "Whoa" as in "Whoa, Nellie," because he tended to lead them into all kinds of mischief and they had to hold him back. The last time Rem had seen him, they'd both lived in Raleigh, Nelson finishing his last year at NC State and Rem concluding his first. Nelson had graduated with a degree in accounting. What had happened to make him into a preacher?

Too curious to leave, Rem waited patiently through the ten-minute graveside ceremony. When it was finished, he picked up his bike and eased toward Nelson. The crowd quickly broke up, and only Nelson and an elderly woman remained. Nelson steered the woman to a black car right behind the hearse and helped her in. Then he turned around and took a deep breath. Rem approached him as the black car with the elderly woman eased away.

"Nelson Hart?" Rem called.

Nelson's eyes narrowed as Rem drew closer.

"It's Rem Lincoln," Rem said.

Nelson moved his way. "What in the world are you doing here?" he asked, sticking out a hand.

Rem vigorously shook the hand, then stepped back. "Riding," he said, indicating his bike. "Home for Christmas, needed some exercise."

Nelson laughed loudly and pointed at Rem's pants and bike shoes. "Most folks don't come to the cemetery dressed like that."

Rem laughed. "Guess not. I didn't plan it, but at least they're black." He pointed toward his mother's grave. "My mom . . . she's buried over there."

Nelson became more serious. "I didn't know," he said.

"Four years ago," Rem said. "Heart disease."

Nelson nodded. "Where you living now?" he asked.

"In Atlanta. I'm in software development."

"I read that Atlanta's a good place for technology development."

"Not so good the last couple of years."

"Read that too."

Rem laughed but not happily. Software development in 2004 spelled disaster for lots of folks, and he wasn't immune to the problems associated with it. Not wanting to think about his troubles, he focused on Nelson again. "Who you burying?" he asked. "Anybody I know?"

Nelson shook his head. "A ninety-year-old man. Been in a nursing home in Hendersonville for years. His family brought him back here for burial. I didn't know him."

"What are you doing in Hilltop? And a preacher too? Last time we were together, you had just taken a job with a big accounting firm in Charlotte."

Nelson shook his head. "The Lord moves in mysterious ways," he said. "I'm the pastor of the Hilltop Community Church now, started close to two years ago."

"My mom went to that church!" Rem said. "Why didn't I know this?"

"You're telling on yourself, you know," Nelson said. "You obviously haven't been home much. Or in church either."

"I'm not a big fan of preachers," Rem said. "Your company the exception, of course."

"Why not?"

"It's a long story."

Nelson shrugged, and Rem felt a little guilty. His mom

wouldn't like his attitude about religion, Lord rest her soul. "What happened to 'Whoa, Nellie'?" he asked.

Nelson waved him off. "Maybe I'll tell you about it someday."

"That'd be good. What you doing tonight? I'll buy you dinner."

"No need for that," Nelson said. "I'm married now. You come to my place, and Julie and I will give you a meal you won't forget for a while. Bring your wife too if you have one."

"No wife," Rem said. "Can't find anybody to have me."

"Then all the more reason for you to come to our place. Expect you don't eat much home-cooked food."

"I can't believe you're married," Rem said. "'Whoa, Nellie' settled down. A sure sign the apocalypse is upon us."

Nelson chuckled. "Julie's great. I met her in California when I went out there for seminary."

Rem chuckled. "You're full of surprises, aren't you?"

"Come to dinner with us. I'll tell you all about it."

Rem paused, a weird feeling popping up. "You won't try to convert me, will you?" he asked, half mocking.

Nelson's face went blank, and Rem couldn't read him.

"You need converting?" Nelson asked.

"No more than you when we were at State together," Rem countered.

"If that's the case, you're in worse shape than you know."

Although Nelson smiled as he spoke, Rem had the

distinct feeling that his tone had suddenly shifted, that his words carried some truth he didn't want to say straight out. A quick fear ran through Rem, and he felt a little uncomfortable with the idea of going to Nelson's. His old friend had obviously changed in the last decade, and the kinds of changes he'd made were complicated, maybe too much for Rem to handle at a time like this.

Rem kicked the ground. "Let me check with my dad," he said. "See what he's got planned for tonight. With so little time at home . . ."

"I understand," Nelson said. "You need to be with your dad as much as possible. Why don't you talk to him, then call me at the church. I'll tell Julie to throw an extra piece of chicken in the pan. If you can't make it, I'll eat it."

"Sounds good," Rem said.

"All right." Nelson stuck out his hand. Rem suddenly remembered something, and an idea floated up. "You think Julie could throw on two pieces of chicken?" he asked.

"Sure," Nelson said. "You hungry?"

"I might bring somebody with me," Rem said. "If that's all right."

"Anybody I know?"

"Let me check," he said. "Maybe so, but I don't want to go out on a limb before I know if it's sturdy."

"Just call me."

"I'll do it."

Nelson opened his arms, and Rem quickly gave his old friend a bear hug and then turned away and hopped on his bike. As he left the cemetery, his mind buzzed a million miles an hour. Jenna was a member of Nelson's congregation, but did that mean she'd go to dinner with him?

Back on the highway, he decided to cut short his ride and go straight home. If he wanted to ask Jenna to dinner, he probably needed to do it as soon as possible. Otherwise she'd think him rude. But wait a minute. Everybody knew her religious inclinations. Was he setting himself up for a lot of Jesus talk if he took Jenna to a preacher's house?

No, he figured as he worked his way up the incline. He'd keep it light, easy, nothing too serious. If Nelson steered matters too deeply toward religion, he'd just bring up "Whoa, Nellie," open a few pages of that old book. That'd shut Nelson up real fast, no doubt about it.

Although pleased he had an escape if needed, Rem found it difficult to relax. This whole trip to Hilltop suddenly felt weird, like a scene from *The Twilight Zone*. He could almost hear Rod Serling from the old television show now—"Three old friends come together for the first time in over ten years in a secluded mountain town at Christmas. What strange current of the universe has brought them together for this fateful rendezvous, and what will happen to their lives as a result of it?"

First, he'd run into Jenna Newsome, now Nelson Hart. What other surprises could this Christmas hold?

∞ 5 ∞

As she'd done nearly every day since she moved back to Hilltop, Jenna stopped by her mom's house right after closing down the day care. To her surprise, as she stepped out of the car, she found her dad, Henry, sitting on the front steps, his tall frame bundled in a black wool coat and leather gloves, his face red with early-evening cold.

"What are you doing?" she called as she moved to him.

He chuckled but didn't stand. "She won't let me inside," he said.

Jenna shook her head at her mom's childish behavior. The last few years had seen all kinds of such craziness from both her parents. If God gave a prize for the most annoying ex-spouse in history, her mom and dad would end up in a dead tie.

"How long you been here?" she asked.

"Close to an hour, I guess. I brought you this." Henry reached to his side and handed her a large box wrapped in bright green paper. "Wanted you to have it on Christmas Eve. Didn't know if I'd see you before then."

"Why didn't you just go to my apartment and wait there?"

He dropped his eyes. "I brought her something too." He picked up another wrapped box and showed it to Jenna. "Wanted to give it to her myself, apologize, you know."

Jenna's heart softened a little, and she gave her dad a quick hug. "Let's go in," she said. "I'll get you a cup of coffee, warm you up some."

"She'll scream to high heaven if I go in," he said. "You deliver her present for me. I'll wait here until you're done, and then we'll go to your place and visit for a while. You know I don't like to create a scene."

"Sure you do," Jenna said. "You love a scene, both of you. Remember her birthday party?"

Henry smiled sheepishly. "That's why I brought her a present."

Jenna eyed her dad; he made her insane sometimes, made her feel like a mom who needed to spank her son. In October she'd made the mistake of inviting him to her mom's birthday dinner at a local restaurant. He'd insisted on bringing the cake, his "peace offering," as he called it. Close to thirty people—all of her mom's best friends—had gathered to celebrate her fifty-fifth year. When everyone had finished eating, the waitress brought out the cake. Seventy-five candles burned on its chocolate surface.

Her mom, Margaret, had always been a stern woman. Her face had tightened slightly at the joke, but she didn't say anything. But then she tried to blow out the candles.

She tried three times before she caught on to the second part of Henry's foolishness. The candles were the kind you couldn't blow out. Margaret's face got red, but she again held her tongue.

Watching her mom, Jenna's blood pressure went up. She knew Margaret didn't do well with much humor, especially her dad's sophomoric kind. Jenna glanced at Henry, but he just shrugged, a good old boy having a few laughs. Jenna hoped the jokes had ended for the night. But Henry had one more round of silliness up his sleeve. When her mom tried to cut the cake, it squeaked.

Jenna's face bleached white. Her mom again applied the knife to the cake. The cake squeaked once more. The crowd laughed nervously. They knew that Henry's offbeat humor and Margaret's straight-laced manners didn't always mix well.

Margaret glared at Henry as he roared with laughter. Jenna grabbed the knife and tried to slice the cake but quickly realized it was Styrofoam covered with chocolate icing. She pointed her finger at her dad, but he didn't seem to care. He'd pulled his prank; he looked happy.

Furious with embarrassment, Margaret had rushed from the restaurant, and although they lived in the same town and saw each other quite often, she'd not spoken to Henry since. No wonder she wouldn't let him inside the house, even to receive a Christmas present.

"You two drive me nuts," Jenna said.

"I know," Henry said. "I'm sorry for that, but you know how she is—so stuffy. I have to stick a pin in her balloon every now and again, just to see the air rush out. You go on in. I'll see you at your apartment."

"Maybe that's wise."

He kissed her, handed her both boxes, and left. After he pulled away, Jenna turned back and went inside. Her mom stood at the window and watched Henry's car as it drove off.

"The man's lost the last marble he ever had," Margaret said.

"You're both loony," Jenna said. "He left this for you." She handed her mom the gift, but she sniffed at it and stalked toward the den.

Jenna followed her, both presents still in hand. Gas logs burned in the fireplace but gave off little heat. Her mom sat down on a brown leather sofa by the fireplace. After putting the gift boxes by the expensive artificial tree that sat opposite the fireplace, Jenna took a seat across from her mom. Her mom wore a pair of pleated gray slacks, a green turtleneck wool sweater, and a pair of stud pearl earrings. Her lipstick looked freshly applied and her makeup as prim as if put on by a professional. As always, every dyed hair on her head lay exactly in place. If Jesus came in the middle of the night, her mom would fall out of bed to meet him looking like the front of *Mature Woman* fashion magazine.

"I wish you two would try to get along," Jenna said. "You've been divorced over six years, should have come to terms with each other by now."

"He's a baby," her mom said, nose high. "Never has grown up."

Jenna sighed and suddenly felt weary of the familiar arguments and age-old hostilities. She had heard the story so many times, always from her mom. Her mom had come from an established Asheville family—people with land handed down through several generations.

Margaret's father, an attorney at the city's leading law firm, had once served as mayor of that big mountain city and chair of the elders at the main street Episcopal church. The Cliburns were as close to aristocrats as most mountain people ever saw.

Her dad had originated from the opposite side of the tracks, from a crossroads about fifteen miles outside of Winston-Salem. Her mom had met him in a freshman English class at UNC—a handsome boy with a slouch in his wide shoulders and a shock of black hair falling into his brown eyes. He laughed easily, and his carefree ways attracted her at the time, a welcome break from the stodgy atmosphere her mother and father maintained at home. He came from a long line of common laborers, not a dime anywhere, but he planned to change that, and she liked the energy his ambition created. The twinkle in his eye delighted her too, and the string of practical jokes he carried out on his friends just came with the package. Her mom thought all of that was exciting before the marriage.

Within weeks after the wedding though, she began to see his humor as mostly out of place. After all, a family man shouldn't act like a schoolboy, should he? A family man had duties to assume, responsibilities that called for a more straight-laced approach.

Henry's goofy humor hadn't been the worst of his offenses though. In fact, Margaret often told Jenna she might have managed to accept his silliness if he had done the right thing regarding a couple of other matters. Like his choice of career after he completed his business degree. Margaret's father offered him a perfectly wonderful position as office manager at his law firm.

To her mother's horror, however, Henry refused to take it. Even worse, he eagerly informed Margaret that he'd already accepted a job with a real estate firm in a place called Hilltop.

"You're kidding me, right?" Margaret had pleaded. "I can't live anywhere but Asheville!"

"Why should I live in Asheville?" Henry asked. "Ride your daddy's coattails? I want to make my own way."

Margaret argued, but to no avail. What else could she do? She couldn't cause a stink so soon after the wedding. Her pliant mother had taught her that. "The man leads," her mother had often said. "The woman's duty is to follow."

"But what if he's leading you over a cliff?"

"You find ways to redirect the trip. But you can't ever let him know you're doing the guiding."

Too young to know how to do that, Margaret had no choice but to move to Hilltop. For a couple of years, she thought she'd die there. To make it worse, Henry refused to accept any money from her parents to help in their transition.

"I'll not live on your father's dole," Henry kept repeating when her folks sent them a check and he mailed it back. "I'll not be obligated to them."

Margaret always pressed him. "You wouldn't have to work such long hours if you'd accept their generosity," she pleaded, upset at all the time she spent alone, even on weekends. "You could come home at a decent hour."

"Look," he pleaded. "I know your dad came home at 5 p.m. every day. And I've never seen him do a thing for his work on a weekend. But he's got that luxury. His family spent decades building a business; all he's got to do is hold it in line. He's hired other people to handle the after-hours stuff. I don't have that."

"But you could," she argued. "I'm sure dad will set you up with a real estate company in Asheville if that's what you want."

Henry shook his head, and the dispute became an ongoing point of difference between them. Year after year he hustled all over, taking appointments at all hours of the day and night. Margaret spent a lot of time home alone, her reserved temperament and slightly snobby ways keeping her from making friends fast or easily.

Gradually, Henry built his business into a successful venture. As he did, he moved them through a succession of houses until they finally bought the nice two-story brick place on close to twenty acres where Margaret still lived. Just as gradually, Margaret made some friends and became a pillar of the community—chairwoman of the Ladies' League, head of the Hospitality Committee at the Community Church, member of the Garden Club. Although quiet around strangers, Margaret slowly loosened up, and people came to know they could depend on her. Without planning it, she sank roots into the mountain soil.

Henry's business boomed in the eighties and nineties as people from all over the country, seeking quiet living, moved into the county. Yet no matter how much money he made, real estate earnings always made Margaret feel slightly soiled, like it didn't count as much if it didn't come from an old family mattress somewhere.

Looking back on it, Jenna knew that both parents carried blame for the failure of their marriage. In many ways, her dad never did grow up. On the other hand, her mom never really relaxed. The things they'd liked about each other at the beginning became the things they also hated. Perhaps they were doomed from the start.

Gradually, the problems mounted. Margaret continued to press Henry to move to Asheville, but he stayed firm in saying no. He kept asking her to have more children, but she told him she felt fine with the one they had. She stopped laughing at his jokes. That just seemed to spur him toward more craziness. She poured her time into community charities. He worked longer hours. She resented him. He ignored her.

Then Margaret's father died, and she tried one more time to make Henry move. "My mother needs me," she kept repeating.

"You live twenty miles away," Henry said. "Go see her every day if you want. But we're not moving."

The space between them grew wider. One day Henry came home and found his clothes moved out of their room to a smaller bedroom down the hall. In retaliation, one day when Margaret went to see her mom, he called in some painters and had her bedroom painted pink. To get back at him, Margaret spent a lot of money but refused to keep up with checkbooks or receipts. So Henry stopped depositing money to her account. Margaret failed to tell him when people called requesting information about property. He decided to make Saturday night a poker night at their house with ten of his best buddies.

Finally, twenty-six years after their wedding, the day came when neither of them could take it anymore, and they divorced. To everyone's surprise, Margaret chose to stay in Hilltop after it ended. "I've made my peace with this place," she explained. "Might as well stay now."

Although wanting to believe her, Jenna suspected her mom had stayed to bedevil Henry too, to make sure he didn't have free rein to say whatever he wanted about her after she'd left.

Now, almost seven years later, the bickering continued and Jenna felt caught right in the middle. She wished once more she'd never moved back to Hilltop. But what choice did she have?

"How's the Strack boy?" her mom asked, breaking the silence and bringing Jenna back to the moment.

"Not good. I'm afraid we're not going to make it."

"The paper says you still need over two hundred thousand dollars."

"We've got a long way to go."

"I'll give five thousand," her mom said.

Jenna's mouth dropped for a second, but then she caught herself. Her mom did a lot of charitable things, usually when you least expected it.

"That's generous," she said softly. "I'm sure the family will appreciate it."

"I don't want them to know it was from me," she said. "Just write me down for the pledge."

"You're a kind woman," Jenna said.

"I do have a heart. Though I think you and your dad sometimes forget that."

Jenna smiled. "You do keep us guessing," she said.

"You headed to the hospital in a while?" Margaret asked.

"Eventually," Jenna said.

"You spend more time with the Stracks than you do with me."

Jenna scowled at the turn in her mom's tone but wasn't surprised by it. "I come by here every day," Jenna said.

"You don't stay long."

"I wonder why."

"That's not a nice thing to say."

Jenna's blood pressure rose as she saw the familiar pattern start to play out. Her mom had just done a nice thing by pledging the five thousand dollars. But then she'd shifted, made a statement to make Jenna feel guilty in an effort to control her. Jenna had resented it and said something mean in return. Her mom had become a victim, the poor injured mom just trying to stay close to her daughter.

"I'm going to leave now," Jenna said, "before we both say something we'll regret this close to Christmas. I'll call you later."

"Go on then." Margaret sniffed. "You always run; it's your best thing."

Jenna's anger boiled, and she almost took the bait but then realized that Henry's appearance had upset her mom, made her even more sensitive than usual. She stepped to Margaret and put a hand on her shoulder. "I'll call you when I get home," she said. "And thanks again for the donation."

Margaret shrugged, and Jenna headed to the door. As she opened it, Margaret spoke. "You got a phone call this morning," she said. "A man."

Jenna turned back. "Reverend Hart?"

"No, somebody I didn't know."

"He leave a name?"

"Rem, I think. You know him?"

Jenna shut the door and faced her mom. "From a long time back," she said. "He's Roscoe Lincoln's son. I went to high school with him."

"Why is he calling you?"

"You'd have to ask him that. I'm surprised you didn't."

"Don't get smart with me."

"He leave a number?"

"No."

"You tell him when you'd see me?"

"No."

"Did you give him my work number?"

"No. He didn't ask, and I saw no reason to volunteer it."

Jenna started to leave but then hesitated. For reasons she couldn't explain, she suddenly wanted to see Rem. "He say if he'd call back?" she asked.

"No."

Jenna leaned against the door frame. The notion of having somebody from outside Hilltop to talk to sure seemed attractive. Of course, she hadn't treated him too well last night . . . but since he'd called, that meant he hadn't let that put him off too much.

Margaret stood and walked Jenna's way. "What's your interest in this man?" she asked.

"He's an old friend," she said. "Nothing more than that."

"Good," Margaret said. "He's here for Christmas, then gone. You don't need to get mixed up with somebody like that. Men are no good; it's best to leave them alone if you can. You don't need them."

Jenna stared at her mom. What did she know about what she needed or didn't need when it came to men?

She thought about calling Rem at his dad's house. Was that too forward? In the old days, yes. But these days, who knew?

Her mom put a hand on her elbow. "You're doing fine without a man," she soothed. "You and me, we're making it okay."

Jenna's eyes suddenly watered. Was she making it okay? She certainly didn't feel like it. She'd messed up at love. No, not at marriage, because no man had wanted her enough to marry her. But love, she'd shown she had no clue about that. And Mickey's situation? She might as well admit she'd never raise enough money for the transplant. Here she was, thirty years old, living in a small apartment in a nowhere town with her stiff, controlling mom and childish dad. What kind of life was this? What did she have to look forward to? Nothing, that's what, and she could see no way to change it.

"I need to go," she said, wiping her eyes.

"I know," Margaret said. "Call me after you get home."

Jenna nodded. Her mom gently brushed back her hair, and Jenna again noted the contrast. Cold, hard in one minute; caring, nurturing in the next. Was she the same way? Was that part of her struggle? She certainly hoped not.

"You'll feel better soon," Margaret said. "Christmas is almost here. You always feel better at Christmas."

Jenna hugged her mom, then walked out. At her car, she paused and stared into the sky. Unless something highly unusual happened this year, not even Christmas would make her feel better this time.

∽6∽

Rem reached Nelson's house just after dark, a bouquet of flowers for Julie on the front seat. He'd thought about bringing a bottle of wine but didn't know how appropriate that was for a preacher. Parking his car, he thought of Jenna and wished he could have reached her. If nothing else, she'd have given him some buffer from any hard-sell conversion efforts Nelson might try. Harder to put the religious squeeze on a guy with somebody else in the room, he figured.

Rem flipped open his cell phone to check his messages one more time as he climbed out but quickly saw that Jenna hadn't called back. Disappointed, he closed the phone and slipped it into his pocket. He'd tried Jenna at her apartment and her mom's house, had left his number on Jenna's answering machine. Obviously, she didn't want to talk to him. He climbed the steps to Nelson's door and started to knock, but the door opened before he could. Nelson stepped outside, a slender redhead at his side.

"Come on in," Nelson said. "Honey, this is Rem Lincoln."

Rem handed Julie the flowers and shook her hand. Julie smelled the flowers. "Nelson tells me you used to be the sane one," she said with a smile. "Says you got him home a few times when he was rather indisposed."

"You mean he's already given you all my blackmail material?"

"I think so."

They all laughed as Julie led them into the house. Rem glanced quickly around. Lots of pictures covered the walls in the entry, most of them nature photographs. Julie led them into a small den area. Again, a variety of nature photographs covered the walls.

"Who's the photographer?" Rem asked, pausing by a striking picture of a hummingbird hovering over a box filled with yellow flowers.

"Nelson," Julie said. "He's a man of many talents."

Nelson pointed Rem to a leather chair. "I took it up when I went to seminary," he said.

"They're amazing," Rem said.

"I enjoy it," Nelson said. "Calms me, and you know I need a lot of calming."

Rem studied his old friend. "I'm real confused," he said with a smirk. "You're a different guy than the one I knew."

"Can you keep a secret?" Nelson asked, looking around as if to make sure no one else heard them.

"Sure."

"I'm not really Nelson," Nelson whispered. "I'm an alien. The real Nelson is on a spaceship out past Mars somewhere."

Rem laughed.

"I need to put these in some water," Julie said, holding up the flowers, "then check dinner."

"It smells great," Rem said, getting a whiff of fried chicken. "You need any help?"

"No, you guys catch up. I'll yell when it's ready."

Rem eased into the chair. Nelson took a spot on a love seat across from him.

"Julie's beautiful," Rem said. "Lots better than you deserve."

"The Lord is still in the miracle-working business," Nelson said.

"Seems so."

"What's new with your love life?" Nelson asked. "Don't remember you having many peers in that department."

"I date a lot," Rem said. "But nobody special right now."

"I figured you to be married by now," Nelson said. "Maybe more than once."

"That's not funny," Rem said in mock offense.

"Don't tell me you're getting sensitive in your old age."

Rem threw a cushion at him.

"Sorry your date didn't work out tonight," Nelson said. "Who'd you ask?"

Rem shrugged. He'd called Nelson earlier and told him he'd be coming solo. "It doesn't matter," he said. "Never did reach her."

The phone rang and Nelson picked it up. Rem stood and studied the wall photos—animals of all shapes and sizes, flowers, mountain streams, sunsets, and sunrises. Nelson seemed to have a gift for photography.

"Hey, Rem?"

Rem faced Nelson, who had the phone mouthpiece covered with one hand. "You mind if we add a fourth to dinner?"

"What's the deal?"

"A friend is asking Julie and me to go get ice cream. But you're here and we can't do that, so I thought maybe we could just ask her over."

"It's a 'her'?"

"Yeah, a woman named Jenna—maybe you know her."

Rem raised an eyebrow. "You didn't set this up, did you?"

"No way!"

Rem did some quick thinking. When he'd left his message on Jenna's machine, he'd said nothing about dinner plans with Nelson. Strange that it had worked out this way, but what difference did it make? He'd have protection from Nelson and get to spend a couple of hours with an attractive woman. What harm could come from that?

"It's fine by me," he said.

Nelson focused again on the phone. Rem wondered if he'd dressed well enough. Pleated khakis, a burgundy crew-neck shirt, casual brown shoes. He felt presentable but not overly so. Nelson hung up the phone.

"I know Jenna," Rem said. "Not that well, but we went to high school together. I saw her at the grocery yesterday."

"She's a quality lady," Nelson said. "A good friend to Julie."

Julie entered and told them to wash up. Within five minutes Rem and Nelson finished in the bathroom and made their way to the dining room table. Just as they took their seats, the doorbell rang and Julie hurried to greet Jenna. Rem's hands suddenly turned clammy, and his tongue felt thick. A few seconds later Julie returned with Jenna, and Rem's stomach flipped as he saw her. Although dressed in a simple pair of black slacks and a cream-colored blouse, she looked great. She wore her hair pulled back on one side, revealing a petite ear and hoop earring, and her eyes seemed bluer tonight than he'd ever seen them.

"I believe you two know each other," Nelson said as Rem stuck out a hand to greet Jenna.

"I tried to call you," Rem said, ignoring Nelson and Julie.

"You don't give up, do you?"

"Not easily."

"You didn't tell me you were coming here for dinner."

"No, I didn't," Rem said.

"This is the girl you tried to ask?" Nelson asked, his voice disbelieving.

"Yeah," Rem said, never taking his eyes off Jenna. "Coincidence, huh?"

"I don't believe in coincidence," Nelson said.

"Come with me to the kitchen," Julie said, grabbing Nelson by the sleeve. "Let these two say hello."

Nelson eyed Rem for a second but then followed Julie out.

Rem faced Jenna and pulled out the seat to his right. "Glad you came," he said, indicating she should take the chair.

71

"I had nothing better to do," she said. "And I didn't know you were here."

"You wouldn't have come if you'd known?"

"Like I said, I had nothing better to do."

Rem slid her chair under her as she sat down. "You look great," he said.

"I've heard flattery before," she said. "It won't work with me."

"Are you always this warm and friendly?"

"I know your reputation," she said. "Remember high school?"

"That was a long time ago."

"You saying you've changed?"

"Not necessarily."

Nelson and Julie came back, their hands full of bowls and trays. "Food's ready," Nelson said. "You two hungry?"

"Starved," Rem said.

"Good," Julie said. "I made enough for a small army."

They put the food down, and Rem inhaled deeply. The smell of chicken, collard greens, corn bread, and mashed potatoes filled his nostrils. From his right, he smelled another aroma also, the subtle scent of Jenna's light perfume. Something in him warmed, and he wanted to lean over and take her hand. But since he knew such a bold move would scare her to death, he reached for the mashed potatoes instead.

⚜

Even though the food tasted delicious, Jenna didn't eat much. Her mind kept swirling through the chain of events that had brought her to this table beside Rem. She'd driven straight home after she left her mom, visited with her dad for a few minutes, and then headed to the Stracks'. To her surprise, she'd found nobody there. After a couple of phone calls, she'd learned that the entire Strack family had gone to the hospital and wouldn't get back for at least an hour. Not wanting to go home to her empty apartment, she'd called Julie to ask her and Nelson out. They'd asked her over for dinner instead, their invitation leaving out the part about Rem's presence.

Slightly perturbed, Jenna stayed quiet through much of the meal as Rem and Nelson laughed and kidded about their days at State. Story after story rolled out of their mouths, and Jenna saw that Nelson genuinely liked Rem and fondly remembered their college days. Strange, Jenna thought, that a godly man like Nelson had ever had much in common with somebody like Rem. Of course, Nelson hadn't always been so godly.

As everybody finished eating, Rem asked Nelson about the changes in his life.

"You sure you want to hear that story?" Nelson asked. "It's a whole lot of religion."

"Give me the Cliff's Notes version," Rem said with a laugh. "Leave out the 'God spoke to me in the still of the night' stuff."

Nelson didn't seem to take any offense. "You know I left State in 1990," he said.

"Yeah, to work on a master's degree."

"Well, I finished that degree in about two years, then took a job with Miller and Thompson, a large accounting firm in Raleigh. I stayed there close to four years."

"Yeah, I saw you a couple of times while you were there. You were a roaring success."

"Truthfully, yes. I moved up fast. Only one problem."

"What was that?"

Nelson dropped his head. "I bent a few rules along the way," he admitted. "We all did. The go-go days, you remember them. Accounting firms all over willing to fudge a few numbers here or there to make their clients happy, to pump up a company portfolio so it would look better to stockholders."

"You got involved in all that?"

"Not directly. I wasn't high enough in the company to do too much damage, just enough to show complicity when the trial came."

Jenna sat up straighter. She'd never heard this story. Nobody in Hilltop had.

"You ended up on trial?" Rem asked.

"I was small potatoes," Nelson said. "But my firm's president and six others ended up charged with a variety of offenses."

"What happened?"

Nelson's face became grim. "Three guys got some prison time," he said. "The president ended up with six years, three suspended. The other two guys got three years, suspended to one. I got a year, suspended, plus three years probation and my CPA license revoked for five years."

"I can't believe it," Rem said.

"I dodged a bullet," Nelson said. "But it got me to thinking, I can tell you that."

"You come to Jesus during the trial?" Rem asked. "Throw yourself on the mercy of the court, is that it?"

"No," Nelson said, not smiling. "Nothing like that. But later, about a month after the trial, I saw a former professor at a coffee shop where I'd taken a part-time job. A man named Johnson, retired. He toddled in, bought a cup of coffee, told me he remembered me from his business class, had read about me and the trial in the paper. I told him I was sorry I had disappointed him. He wanted to know what I planned to do next."

"What did you tell him?" Rem asked.

"I told him I didn't know. He asked me if I had ten minutes, said he'd like to buy me a cup of coffee. I said, 'Sure, why not.' We took a table, and Johnson asked me if I knew that what I had done was wrong. I told him yes, I knew.

"'Then why did you do it?' he asked."

"What'd you tell him?" Rem asked.

"I told him I didn't have a clue. The money, the excitement—who knows why anybody does stupid things?" Nelson put his coffee on the table. "The next thing Johnson said changed my life."

"What was that?" Rem asked.

"He told me I had no anchor."

"What?"

"An anchor. Johnson said I didn't have one. Said he'd seen it a thousand times. A smart guy comes through the business school. All the talent in the world, but he's got no grounding, nothing to keep him steady, solid in who he is when the temptations come."

"Dr. Johnson invited Nelson to church," Julie said.

"Jesus is the anchor, is that it?" Rem asked, his tone shifting slightly toward sarcasm.

Nelson nodded. "I believe so. Came to that conclusion about three months after Johnson bought me coffee. I did a lot of investigation during that time, studied Christian teaching, its history, its traditions, its Scriptures. I started it as an intellectual discipline, figured it couldn't hurt, and I had plenty of time. By the time I finished, my heart had changed. Nothing all of a sudden, no real emotion to it, just a calm assurance that the Jesus I'd studied for the last few months was real, present, ready to accept me, forgive me, change me."

"I liked you the way you were," Rem said.

Nelson laughed. "That way almost landed me in prison."

"He visited California soon after that," Julie said. "To visit an uncle he hadn't seen in a long time."

"He lived near Fuller Seminary in Pasadena," Nelson said. "I stayed with him that summer after the trial. Heard a Fuller professor, an ethics guy, at his church, a man who talked about how every person, no matter what they did, should make their vocation an offering to God. I planned to go back into accounting someday, had no notion to do anything else. But I wanted to hear this professor some more, signed up for a summer course he taught, an ethics introduction class. By the time the summer ended, I knew I couldn't leave the place, the classes, the rigor of the study. Whatever the Lord wanted for me, I would follow. I graduated in three years, served a church while there, first as an associate pastor. Then I got the chance to come home to Hilltop. That's the story."

"All except how you met Julie," Jenna said.

Nelson laughed as he gazed at his wife. "That's another miracle," he said. "Maybe we should save that one for another night."

Rem leaned back, and Jenna watched to see how he'd respond to Nelson's tale.

"It's hard to believe you're on the God squad now," Rem said.

"I know it seems weird to you," Nelson said. "But have you got a better explanation for the way the world is, the design, the beauty?"

"How do you explain what's not so beautiful?" Rem asked. "Like the little boy Jenna's trying to help. What's his name?" He turned to her.

Jenna tensed as she felt the edge in the question. "Mickey," she said. "Mickey Strack."

"What about him?" Rem asked. "Others like him? What's beautiful about that?"

Nelson glanced at Julie. "I know there's suffering in the world," he said. "And I can't explain it all. But it seems that freedom demands some pain, heartache, some death. Otherwise we're computers with no mind, no heart of our own."

Rem didn't seem convinced.

Nelson tried another approach. "What's the purpose of living if there's not something beyond this life?" he asked.

"Who said there's got to be a purpose?"

"So you think it's all pointless," Nelson said. "All of us, everything that exists. All of it is just pure circumstance, no direction, no meaning?"

"Why not?"

Nelson leaned toward Rem, his hands on his knees. "I could give you a long theological answer," he said, "but I'm not sure this is the time for it. Am I right?"

Rem stared at his shoes. Silence fell for several seconds.

Jenna suddenly felt cold. Was Rem correct? Was everything empty? Her life? The life of everyone in the room? If so, it didn't matter much if Mickey Strack lived or died. His life and the lives of all those who loved him were in vain.

"Who wants dessert?" Julie asked, obviously seeking to lighten the mood. "We've got bread pudding."

"I'll help you get it," Jenna said.

In the kitchen, Julie picked up a tray, poured four cups of coffee, sat the cups on the tray, and faced Jenna. "Rem is fun," she said.

"You think so?"

"Don't you?"

"He seems like trouble to me."

"Is that why you've been so quiet?"

"I wanted to let him and Nelson talk," Jenna said.

"Rem's searching right now; you can see it written all over him."

"That's why I tried to leave it between him and Nelson," Jenna said. "I didn't want to mess things up."

"He likes you," Julie said. "Might not hurt you to loosen up a little, make him feel a bit more welcome."

"So you're Ann Landers now?"

Julie shrugged, sat a cup of cream and a sugar bowl on her tray, and led Jenna back into the den where Nelson and Rem stood by the fireplace, Rem with a piece of wood in hand, Nelson with a metal prod stoking up the embers.

"Men make fire," Julie teased.

"Women bring dessert and coffee," Nelson countered.

Julie sat the tray on a flat table and pointed Jenna to the sofa in front of it as Nelson and Rem finished getting the fire going. A couple of minutes later, the two men took chairs across from Jenna. Julie joined Jenna on the sofa. Nelson picked up a cup of coffee and sipped from it. The room suddenly felt cozy, and Jenna decided maybe Julie was right. She needed to loosen up. She glanced at Rem and saw him staring at her, and she blushed. He grinned and she smiled back, a warm sense of pleasure seeping into her bones. Apparently the serious conversation had ended, and Jenna felt better. For the first time in far longer than she wanted to admit, a handsome, successful, single man seemed interested in her. Maybe this Christmas would turn out okay after all.

᳒᳐᳑

For close to an hour, Rem stayed with Nelson, Julie, and Jenna, his nerves relaxing as the conversation moved away from matters of religion. After everyone had finished their bread pudding, Julie and Jenna disappeared into the kitchen with the dishes, and Nelson and Rem remained alone. The fire crackled. Rem relaxed into the sofa.

"What do you think of Jenna?" Nelson asked.

"You're a matchmaker now?"

"You seem to need some help."

"She's a little quiet," Rem said. "But I won't hold that against her."

"She's a sensitive woman," Nelson said, serious again. "Please don't trifle with her."

"I'm just home for Christmas," Rem said. "That's not enough time to trifle with anyone."

"My point exactly."

79

Julie and Jenna returned, Julie moving to Nelson, Jenna to the seat across from Rem. Rem's cell phone rang. For a second he thought about ignoring it but then realized he couldn't take the chance. Pulling out the phone, he turned his back to the group and cupped the phone to his ear.

"Yeah," he said.

"Rem, you got a minute?"

He recognized the voice of Lisa Toller, his business partner. "What's up?" he asked.

Lisa hurriedly outlined the situation. Rem stood and moved to a window across from the fireplace.

"You need to get back here," Lisa concluded. "If this is going to happen, it's got to go down before Christmas."

"I'm with my dad," Rem said. "You sure we can't wait? Take a little more time to make a decision?"

"You know we can't. Everybody scatters for Christmas, and we won't get them together again until after New Year's. One way or the other, you've got to decide before then. They want it closed this year for tax purposes."

Rem rubbed his forehead. He didn't like feeling under the gun like this, the squeeze of having to make a decision. Yet that's one reason he'd come home this year, to get some distance from his problem, some objectivity. He'd hoped coming to Hilltop would provide that but now wondered if he'd done the right thing. Maybe he should have stayed in Atlanta, kept his hand on the pulse of things.

"What's your gut telling you?" he asked Lisa.

"Not for me to say," she said. "You're the boss."

He rubbed his head again. "Okay," he finally said.

"Get the papers ready. I'll catch an 8 a.m. flight from Asheville; meet me at the airport. We'll take one more look at things, then see if we can get this settled."

"Sounds like a plan."

"See you then."

He hung up and turned back to the group. "Sorry," he said. "Business."

"You can't even get off for Christmas?" Jenna asked.

"Pressing matters," he said.

"He's a software tycoon," Nelson said. "Haven't you heard? A big shot in computer circles. Have you seen his car? That watch he wears? The man's got money, I tell you."

"I need to go," Rem said. "I've had a great time."

Jenna's face fell, and Rem thought he saw disappointment in it. Although he liked that, it bothered him too. Why should his leaving bother her? They barely knew each other.

"It's still early," Julie said. "Only ten."

"I have to leave by six or so tomorrow to get a flight to Atlanta," he explained. "A meeting at noon."

"I guess you are a tycoon," Jenna said.

"Sorry," he said again. "But nobody can schedule a crisis."

"You think you'll get back before Christmas?" Nelson asked.

"Hope so, but I'm not sure."

"I want you to come to Christmas Eve services."

"I don't know about that," Rem said.

"Why not?"

Rem stared at the floor. How could he explain without hurting Nelson's feelings? "Look," he said, looking back up. "I've had a great time tonight. But . . . well . . . let me say this honestly . . . preachers aren't my favorite people. I told you that at the cemetery."

"I'd like to hear about that."

"Maybe you will someday, but not now. Not enough time."

"It sounds serious."

"I guess it is."

Nelson didn't press him. "Hope to see you before Christmas anyway."

Rem smiled. "I plan to come back; need to spend Christmas with my dad. He's not that well."

"If you change your mind, services are at 11 p.m. Christmas Eve."

"I'll remember that."

"You better."

Rem turned to Jenna. "I'll follow you home," he said.

"It's not necessary."

"I know, but I'd like to do it."

Jenna shook her head. "I think I'll stay here a little longer. You go on."

"I had a nice time," Rem said.

"Take care," she said.

"Okay." Rem stared at her for several seconds, lost in her eyes. How blue they were. How kind too, although a little haunted these days, far more so than the first time he'd seen them so long ago. He wanted to remind her of that day, wanted to ask her if she remembered, wanted to . . .

He shook his head against the notion. She didn't

remember, never had. Not back in high school when he moved to Hilltop and certainly not now.

"Can I call you when I get back?" he asked.

"If you'd like."

He smiled at her one more time, then left.

In his car, he took a deep breath, held up his hands, and saw they were trembling slightly. He grabbed the steering wheel to still them. An odd feeling ran through him, and he tried to shake it off. What was going on here? He looked back at Nelson's house and marveled again at how different Nelson seemed, so settled, so peaceful, so content.

Rem cleared his throat and started the car. Content—not exactly how he'd describe his own life right now. Pulling from the driveway, he focused on what he needed to do to get ready for his meeting the next day. No time for anything but that, he decided. No time for anything else at all.

∞7∞

Rem landed in Atlanta at just after nine the next morning, his body wired by three cups of airplane coffee. His partner, Lisa, a late-twenties free spirit with closely cut black hair, purple lipstick, and red-rimmed glasses, met him at the terminal.

"The meeting is set," she said as they hurried toward her car. "You know yet what you're going to do?"

Rem shook his head. "It's not just me," he said. "You've got almost as big a stake as I do. Whatever we do, we'll do together."

"But you own 60 percent," she said.

"Doesn't matter. You disagree with my choice, we don't do it."

They reached the car—a three-year-old Volvo with an empty Starbucks coffee cup in each of the two cup holders between the front seats. Lisa handed him a stack of papers, and he settled into his seat and started reading them as she drove away.

"What are the latest figures on the debt?" he asked.

"Close to four," she said.

"What are they offering?"

"They haven't indicated exactly."

Rem studied the papers as Lisa paid the parking attendant and headed north up Interstate 85. "You think they'll offer six?" he asked. "That would give us enough to settle our debts and clear a little for the two of us."

"No way to tell."

Rem pored over the papers for the next ten minutes. A warm sun gleamed through the windows. As they neared Atlanta's skyline, he laid down the papers and looked up. "How long we been at this?" he asked Lisa, his mood reflective.

Lisa glanced at him, then back to the highway. "You mean this last venture or since we started out?"

"All totaled."

"We met at State," she said, her mood shifting with his. "Computer lab, senior year."

"You tried to hit on me," Rem said, smiling.

"I did not!" Lisa said. "Just the opposite! But I never responded to your feeble efforts."

"It didn't help me that you and Taylor were six months away from the altar."

"We started working on a software program," Lisa said.

"It standardized a way for hospitals to track their medicines—purchasing, shipping, receiving. Took three years after graduation to get the bugs out," Rem recalled. "Then we sold it. Wonder if we sold too soon?"

"Probably."

Lisa left the interstate and headed toward downtown Atlanta. "If we'd waited until '98 or '99, we probably could have gotten ten times as much," she said.

"We thought four million was plenty," Rem said.

"Yeah, all the money we'd ever need." She drove toward a parking garage.

Rem put his papers back in the briefcase. "You think we've goofed up?" he asked. "Sold the first program too early, and now waited too late on this one?"

Lisa parked and faced him, her brown eyes kind but firm. "We're smart people," she said. "Whether we sold too early or not, I have no clue. But this last thing, it wasn't ready until now and we both know it. We've invested the money we made from our first program in this one, plus we've had to go in some debt. But, hey, there's not a lot of venture capital out there these days. You do what you have to do. Now we've got an offer. We don't know how much yet, and we have a choice to make. That's the situation, we'll handle it. No worries."

Rem sighed. Lisa was right. Their latest program—a software package that enhanced a computer's ability to recognize and delete unwanted email before it ever entered a person's mailbox—gave them a chance to pay off their debts and maybe earn a few bucks as well. Maybe they should wait a while longer to sell, but theirs wasn't the only such program out there, and waiting might mean disaster. What if somebody else put out a better system while they waited on a higher bid?

"What if their offer isn't enough?" he asked.

"What's enough?" Lisa asked.

"I don't know. But I've gotten accustomed to a certain lifestyle. You too. If they offer just enough to pay off our debts, we'll have nothing left."

"You can always make more money," Lisa said. "That's the great thing about computers. If you're smart enough, you can always come up with something new. We've done it twice, we can do it again."

He smiled at her. "You're my inspiration," he said.

"Let's go check these numbers again before the meeting," she said.

They left the car, Rem's head aching from tension over the decision he faced.

∽✦∼

The morning at the Kid's Delight Day Care passed with no more trauma than normal. One child threw up and Jenna sent for her parents to come get her, and a little boy bit his neighbor at the coloring table, but that was about it for drama. Jenna sat down in her small office about 11:30, took a sip of water from the bottle she usually kept close by, and looked forward to closing for Christmas for the next four days. She needed the break. Between directing the day care and leading the efforts for Mickey's Miracle, she felt like a welcome mat an army had marched on.

Leaning back for a few moments, her thoughts drifted to the previous night, and she found herself thinking of Rem. Would he come back before Christmas? Would she see him again over the holidays? After the way she'd treated him, probably not. Should that bother her? Absolutely not! She'd decided a long time ago to stay away from faithless men, and he'd given ample evidence last night that not only did he have no faith, but he actually felt a little hostile toward Christian people.

She wondered about the source of that hostility. Not his mother, that was for sure. She'd spent a lot of time in church, sang in the choir, served in the nursery, held the president's position in the Ladies' Missions Society. How could a son fall so far from his mom's beliefs? Of course, Rem's dad didn't come to services too often either. Guess Rem took after him.

Jenna rocked forward and squared her shoulders. No time to worry about Rem Lincoln. For all she knew, she'd see him again in about ten years, just like this time. She reached for a pen to sign some papers she needed to mail but then heard footsteps and looked up to see Tom Strack stepping through the door. Tom looked frazzled, his eyes wide, a baseball cap in his hand. Brenda trailed him, her face white and scared. Suddenly fearful, Jenna stood and hugged Brenda, then pointed both her and Tom to the two chairs facing her desk.

"What's up?" she asked, although not sure she really wanted to know. "How's Mickey today?"

"That's why we're here," Tom said. "The hospital . . . they . . ." He dropped his eyes, and Jenna looked to Brenda.

"The hospital administrator came this morning," Brenda said, "all apologetic but with bad news. He said they'd spent all they could on Mickey's care, almost forty thousand dollars so far. Their bosses up the line said we had to pay it or leave."

"Say that again." Jenna couldn't believe her ears. Nobody could act so badly.

"It's true," Tom said, squeezing the bill of his cap. "We were planning to take Mickey home for Christmas day. He's well enough for that, Dr. Russell already told us. But they told us today we couldn't bring him back afterward, said they couldn't do anything else for him here anyway."

"I'm confused," Jenna said. "Dr. Russell said we could keep Mickey there as long as we needed until the transplant."

Brenda nodded. "That's right," she said. "But . . . well . . . the hospital is owned by a health-care group in Nashville, and they've got a new regional administrator in Asheville. Least that's what we're told. They only allow so much for folks who can't pay, and we've reached that and then some. Besides . . ." She looked to Tom as if to ask him to continue the explanation.

"They don't think we'll get the money for the transplant," Tom whispered.

"What?"

Tom looked like a man facing a hanging. "They know how much money we've raised," he said. "And Mickey's situation has gotten so bad that if we don't get the transplant within a few weeks, they know it'll be too late. But they don't see how we can get the money in time."

"So they're just putting him out with nowhere to go?" Jenna asked, her heart breaking.

"Dr. Russell said he'd come by the house every day," Brenda said, her eyes filling with tears. "Said if we couldn't . . . get the transplant, we . . . we might as well make Mickey comfortable at home. Keep him near us. He said he'd prescribe any medicine he needed to keep him out of pain, would charge it to his practice." She wiped her eyes, but it didn't do much good.

Jenna turned to Tom, but he didn't look at her. She wanted to scream and tell them she wouldn't let this happen, but she felt powerless and knew she had no more options to offer. "I can't believe this is real," she said. "Not after we worked so hard, after people gave so much."

Tom stood, walked to her, and put a hand on her shoulder. "You did everything you could," he said. "We thank you for that. You poured your heart into this. Guess it just wasn't meant to be."

Jenna looked up at him, her eyes wet. Could she just let it go like this? Could she let Mickey's last hope drop? It didn't seem possible.

"How long . . . ?" She couldn't finish the sentence.

Tom squeezed his hat again. "Dr. Russell doesn't know," he said. "I asked him, and he said maybe six weeks, maybe a year. It all depends on whether Mickey catches anything that can . . . well, you know."

Jenna nodded. It all depended on whether Mickey's defenseless body caught any disease that could kill him. She wiped her eyes and tried to accept the defeat. She'd done all she could, but the end of the effort had surely come.

"We'll give the hospital the money we've raised," she said. "They'll take Mickey back if we do that, won't they?"

Tom looked at Brenda. "I expect so," he said. "But that means the transplant is out for sure."

"I know," Jenna said. "But . . . well . . . it's too late in a few weeks anyway. This way Mickey can get the treatment he needs, at least for a while. If he's in the hospital, he'll have a better chance to stay shielded from infections. That'll give us longer to do something else, figure something out."

"You think there's something else we can do?" Tom asked.

Jenna rubbed her eyes. "I don't know. I just don't."

"I hate to give up," Brenda said, still softly crying.

Jenna moved to her and hugged her shoulders. "We all do," she said. "But I'm stumped right now. I need time to think."

Brenda sobbed loudly, her head shaking. Holding her, Jenna tried to stay strong. She'd done all she could. Nobody could blame her for this failure, nobody but herself. Just like when her mom and dad had finally split. Nobody had blamed her, except herself. She'd cried herself to sleep so many nights after her dad moved out, cried into her pillow until her face puffed up and she ran out of tears. She knew now that she had nothing to do with their divorce. Then why did she still feel so guilty?

Brenda lifted her head, and Jenna tried to think of another option for Mickey, but nothing came to her. Without a miracle like none she'd ever seen or dreamed, Mickey would die really fast, and she could do absolutely nothing to stop it. She knew miracles didn't happen, knew because she'd prayed for one at least twice in her life but with no result. No, miracles didn't happen, never had, never would.

⚜

Sitting in his small office, across the table from two men in three-button suits and a woman in a tailored navy pants-and-jacket outfit, Rem drummed his thumb on the table and tried to figure out what to do. The truth was, he didn't want to sell the software program he and Lisa had developed, but he didn't see a way to avoid it. They had more debt than assets, more expenditures than income, and a slew of competitors who might come out any day now with a product that did exactly what theirs did. If he got what he needed, selling made a lot of sense, maybe the only sense.

"Okay," Rem said, gazing steadily at the woman in the navy outfit, a high-powered executive named Holly Stanfield. "You've examined the software; you know the strengths, the weaknesses. It's still got a few bugs, but those are solvable in another couple of months. It's a quality program; we all know that. So let's say we cut to the chase. What's the best offer you can make?"

Stanfield smiled slightly, but Rem kept his face blank. He'd learned in his two other meetings with Stanfield— a woman in her midthirties with a body that looked like she worked out at least two hours a day—that her smile masked a heart as single-minded as a calculator. She liked the facts and nothing but the facts.

"I agree you've written a quality program," Stanfield said. "But you're not the only one trying to do this. We've examined three similar programs in the last two months, all of them also first-rate products."

"I know we've got lots of competition," Rem said. "But if you didn't see something worthwhile in our efforts, you wouldn't be here right before the holidays talking to us. You'd be in somebody else's office making the same speech to them."

Stanfield tilted her head, then leaned to the man next to her and exchanged a few whispers with him. Rem drummed his fingers and wondered if Stanfield was married. She wore no ring, but he knew that didn't always matter these days. Stanfield glanced his way and smiled again, and he sensed that maybe she was flirting with him. He considered the possibilities for a few seconds but then dropped them. Stanfield's smile brought no warmth with it. It seemed more like a painting of a smile than the real thing. The man next to her took an envelope from his suit jacket and handed it to Stanfield. She slowly opened it, pulled out a slip of paper, and slid it across the table to Rem.

Rem took the paper, nodded at Stanfield, and turned to Lisa. He opened the paper and held it so both he and Lisa could see the information printed on it. Keeping his face as blank as possible, he studied the figures for several seconds, then handed the paper to Lisa and looked back at Stanfield. She licked her lips, and he wondered again if she thought her charms could actually make a difference in a business negotiation. Jenna's face suddenly popped into his head, and he held it there for an instant but then pushed it aside. No time for that now.

"It's an interesting offer," he finally said. "Worthy of our appropriate consideration. My partner and I"—he glanced at Lisa—"would like a day or so to mull it over."

Stanfield leaned forward, and all her efforts at charm suddenly disappeared. "We came prepared for a response today," she said. "We hoped we could settle this before we left."

"I know," Rem said. "But as I'm sure you understand, you're talking about something real personal to us—our baby, so to speak. We won't sell that off without proper evaluation."

Stanfield looked at Lisa. "You concur with Mr. Lincoln?"

Lisa nodded.

"I'll give you another twenty-four hours," Stanfield said. "But that's it. This has to be done this year."

"I'm aware of the tax situation," Rem said. "I'll get you an answer before five tomorrow."

"Okay." Stanfield and her companions stood as if controlled by a robotic hand. Rem and Lisa copied them. Stanfield and her associates shook their hands, then left the office.

Rem turned to Lisa. "What do you think?" he asked.

Lisa picked up the paper and studied the number again. "Hard to say," she said. "It all depends on what kind of gamblers we are."

Rem sighed. "I'll call you," he said.

"Tonight?"

"Maybe."

"You're going to your condo?"

"No, back to Hilltop."

Lisa looked a little surprised.

"I can't explain it now," he said. "But I need to go back home."

"You okay?" she asked.

"Sure," he said. "Just a few crazy things going on."

"Your dad's health?"

"No worse than normal."

"Then what is it?"

He started to tell her about Jenna, about meeting Nelson again, about his ride to the cemetery, about the odd feelings he'd had in the last day or so. But how could he? He didn't know what any of it meant, so how could he explain it to somebody else? Suddenly he felt tired, wearier than he'd been in a long time. The notion of selling out and taking some time off appealed to him in ways he'd never dreamed possible.

"We'll talk soon," he said.

"We better," she said.

He hugged Lisa.

She took him back to the airport, and he hopped onboard a plane headed back to Asheville. Looking out the window after takeoff, he tried to relax but couldn't. In the next twenty-four hours he had to make a decision that would change his life forever. And for some strange reason he couldn't fathom, he wanted to talk to Jenna about it before he did anything.

8

Jenna stayed late at the day care that night to make sure everything was in order before she shut down for a week. By the time she'd finished, dark had fallen and everybody else had left. Her bones achy with weariness, she flipped off the last of the lights, locked the doors, pulled on her coat and gloves, and headed to her car. To her surprise, she saw Rem leaning against a Lexus SUV parked next to her Bronco. She stopped in her tracks. "What are you doing here?" she asked suspiciously.

He held up his hands, palms out. "Didn't mean to scare you," he said.

"You didn't," she said. "It's just a shock seeing you here, that's all."

"You seem upset," he said. "I'm not here to bother you. But I flew back in this afternoon and thought I'd ask you to dinner. If that's a problem, I'll just leave."

Jenna hesitated. Why was she acting like this? Although she really didn't trust him, it wasn't like he had two horns growing from the top of his head. But she still saw no reason to have dinner with him. He meant nothing to her, and he'd leave Hilltop in a couple of days and she'd never see him again. Why bother?

"I need to go see my mom," she finally said.

"We can go after that," he offered.

Jenna rubbed her eyes. "I don't understand," she said. "Why are you so interested in me all of a sudden?"

Rem studied her for a few seconds but then sighed and waved both hands in dismissal. "Just forget it," he said. "I won't hassle you anymore." He moved toward his Lexus, and Jenna watched him go.

After he'd climbed in and started the engine, he backed the vehicle up beside her and rolled down his window. His black eyes stood out under the street lamp like twin pieces of coal, and something about them cut into her, trimmed out a piece of her heart. As before, she felt like she'd met him somewhere she'd only visited once, somewhere she wanted to go back and visit again but couldn't remember how to get there.

"I'm sorry you're so scared," he said. "I meant no harm. Just thought the two of us could have a quiet dinner and talk to each other. For some reason I feel like you need that; I know I do."

He sounded wistful, and all of a sudden she felt so alone, so afraid, so brittle that she knew if she didn't talk to somebody, she might just crack into a million pieces on the asphalt parking lot. His window started rolling back up and she did something she didn't quite understand even as she did it. She stepped to the Lexus and knocked on the window. It stopped about halfway up.

"What?" Rem asked, leaning his head out.

"My mom can wait," she whispered. "She's a grown woman."

"You sure?" he asked.

"Yeah," she nodded, suddenly certain. "I'm sure."

"Okay," he said. "Hop in."

She moved to the passenger side. He leaned over to open the door, and she climbed in.

"Where to?" he asked.

"Let's go toward Asheville," she offered. "There's a decent restaurant about ten miles out on I-26."

"Don't want to be seen in Hilltop with me, is that it?"

She studied him to see if he was teasing and decided he was. "Exactly," she said, going along with it. "I have a reputation to protect, you know."

"I hear it's spotless," he said. "I'll have to do something about that."

"Thanks for the warning."

They both laughed, and he directed the Lexus toward Asheville. Leaning back, Jenna thought of her mom and knew she would wonder what had happened to her. For that matter, so did she.

***

Red-and-white checked tablecloths covered the tables at the small restaurant where they ended up, and a large deer head hung over the fireplace. Jenna took off her coat and hung it on one of the wood pegs that stuck out from the wall by the door. Dim lamps lit the room, and people talked softly at their tables. A hostess led them to a booth.

"It's not exactly the Chop House," Rem said as they sat down.

"Why don't you taste the food before you get snobby?" she asked.

"Good idea," he said.

A middle-aged waitress showed up wearing an apron that matched the tablecloth and handed them a couple of menus.

"What's good?" Rem asked.

"I like the steaks," Jenna said.

"You're a carnivore," Rem said. "Let's get a steak then, say a T-bone, just pink in the middle."

"I'll have the petite filet," Jenna said. "Medium rare."

The waitress took the rest of their orders and hustled off.

Rem settled back, and Jenna laid her hands on the table. "I can't believe I'm doing this," she said. "My mom's going to go ballistic."

Rem tilted his head. "I'm a little confused," he said. "You're thirty, close to it anyway, and you're still worried about your mom's reaction when you go out with a man? What's the story with that?"

Jenna studied her hands. "I know it's a little bizarre," she finally said. "But I don't know . . . my mom's got this power over me, this . . . well . . . she stood by me a few years ago when I thought I had nowhere else to go. I can't just forget that now, toss her over. She needs me and I need her. I guess that's the best way to explain it."

The waitress brought them glasses of water. Rem ordered hot tea, then leaned closer to Jenna. "You came back to Hilltop three, four years ago, right?"

"You've heard about that?"

He nodded. "A little. The story in town says some guy broke up with you before the wedding. You want to tell me what happened?"

"Not sure I do."

Rem drank from his water. "I can understand," he said. "But I also expect you've kept it bottled up a long time and had little chance to talk about it. Sometimes it helps though."

"I didn't know you were a psychiatrist."

"Pretend I am."

"You'll be gone the day after Christmas. Why should I tell you anything?"

"Because I'll be gone the day after Christmas. What can it hurt?"

She sipped her water, examined his question, and decided he was right. She had nothing to lose, and it might actually help to get his perspective. "I dated a man for almost four years," she said, her tone empty of emotion. "He owned a couple of car dealerships—one in Winston-Salem, another in Greensboro."

"A man of means."

"Yeah. Handsome, successful, popular, kind, everything a woman wants in a man."

"A churchgoer?"

"Yes. I wouldn't get serious with any other kind of man."

"You've got standards."

"Yes."

The waitress brought their salads. Rem picked up his fork and picked at the lettuce.

"Your guy finally proposed?" he asked.

"On my birthday, after three years."

"Took him long enough."

"I thought so too. We'd been exclusive for over two years."

"But he finally popped the question."

"Yes, then suggested a wedding date about a year off."

"Again, he's mighty slow. If I ever make up my mind to get married, I'm going to make it happen quicker than the first lap of a NASCAR race."

She smiled. "I should have taken his timetable as a hint," she said. "Looking back now, I can see how unsure he was. But then . . ."

"You were in love. Who can blame you?"

She studied him to see if he was teasing, but she couldn't tell. He nibbled on his salad; she ignored hers. "We were three weeks away from the wedding," she said.

"Not quite at the altar," Rem said.

"Close enough," Jenna said. "He called me. I knew something was up the second I heard his voice."

"He didn't meet you face-to-face?"

She shook her head. "He told me he couldn't do it," she said. "He didn't love me. Thought he did, he said, and didn't want to give up on something he'd invested four years of his life in. But he couldn't commit to me. That was it. He hung up."

"That had to leave a mark."

"Like somebody had dropped a minibus on me."

The waitress showed up with their steaks and plopped them down. Rem thanked her, then gave his attention back to Jenna.

"What did you do?" he asked.

"What could I do? I started sending wedding presents back."

"You didn't try to see him, find out what had happened?"

"Oh, I found out all right." She lifted her knife and fork and, fingers trembling, cut into the steak. "He married another woman less than a month later. One of my bridesmaids, a woman who taught school two doors down from me."

"Yikes."

"Yeah." She laid down her fork without eating the steak she'd cut. "I wanted to fillet him like a catfish."

"But you didn't."

"No, I'm too nice. I even sent them a wedding present."

"You're a fine Christian woman."

"Now you're mocking me."

"Maybe so, but you should've had it out with the guy, the woman too. What kind of person does that to somebody?"

Jenna hung her head. "I felt so humiliated," she said. "I couldn't stand to face either one of them. So I just left."

"That's when you came back to Hilltop?"

"Yes, moved in with my mom for a few months, then found the apartment where I live now. Never saw Carl again, Karen either."

"So you've never confronted either one of them?"

"No. I've forgiven them . . . at least tried to."

Rem grunted.

"What?" she asked. "You say I shouldn't?"

"It's not that," he said. "Forgiveness, fine, I agree with that. But my suspicion is you haven't forgiven anybody, not really. You've buried it all instead, covered it up. You ran from Winston-Salem, never told either of them how angry you were, how much they hurt you. You ended up in a cave here in Hilltop, let Mommy take care of you, claimed to have forgiven these two people who've treated you like dirt. But have you? I doubt it. Let me ask you something. How many men have you dated since you moved here?"

"I don't see how that's any of your business," she snapped.

He nodded knowingly. "I bet you haven't dated more than ten men in the last four years," he said. "And probably only a couple of those more than once, and neither of those two as many as five times."

Although furious, Jenna mentally added up the dates she'd had since coming home. To her horror, she realized Rem had guessed correctly. "So what if you're right?" she demanded. "What does it prove?"

He leaned forward, his voice quiet but firm. "I'm not sure," he said. "But I suspect it proves you haven't moved on from Mr. Carl in Winston-Salem. You haven't forgiven him, not really. You're still angry, humiliated, bitter. Otherwise you'd have found someone else by now. I mean . . . look at you . . . you're gorgeous, you're smart, you've got a great heart. But you're not easy to approach; I can tell you that from the last couple of days. You're frosty, like an ice cube on a ski slope."

"Maybe I'm just that way with you," she said.

He grinned. "Maybe, but I'm not willing to believe that."

Jenna thought of her mom, how she seemed so cold sometimes, and wondered if she'd inherited that trait. Pushing away the notion, she addressed Rem again. "Pretty high on yourself, aren't you?"

"I do all right."

She took a drink of water. Was Rem right? She'd tried so hard to forgive Carl and Karen, had prayed about it over and over. Yet when she was honest, she knew she still harbored ill will toward them, Carl especially. What did that mean? How weak her faith must be to have carried this grudge so long, to have let the bitterness lodge so deep.

"I don't know where to go from here," she said. "It's all so confusing."

"I'm sure it is." He took her hands.

Something in the gesture touched her, and she suddenly wanted to cry. A man hadn't held her hands in a long time. His eyes bored into hers, and the same eerie feeling she'd had since she first saw him two days ago returned.

"Sometimes I feel like I've known you a long time," she said. "That I met you before high school . . . I know it's crazy, but . . ." She stopped when she saw the frown on his face. He rubbed her hands gently for at least a minute.

"You did meet me," he finally said, his eyes fixed on her.

She tilted her head, more confused than ever. "When?" she whispered.

He shook his head. "You'll figure it out; we'll talk about it then."

"You sure you're not just handing me a line? You

know, the 'Haven't we met somewhere before?' speech."

"You brought it up first," he said.

Her stomach churned as she tried to remember. Rem's face stayed serious, and the look scared her and she pulled her hands away. "Eat," she said, pointing to his steak. "We don't want these to get cold."

"What's wrong?" he asked. "Don't pull back."

She shook her head. "It's no good," she said. "Mom says you'll be gone the day after Christmas. No reason to . . ."

"To what? To talk to me? To have dinner with me?"

"Yes, I admit it. Mom says it's senseless. Men are trouble, more than they're worth."

"You ever consider you might be listening to your mom too much? That her problems are seeping into your life, coloring your views in ways that aren't healthy?"

"Are you saying she's wrong?"

"I'm saying that anybody can be trouble, men or women. Relationships aren't easy, no matter how you slice them. But are you going to let one awful experience make you a nun? Let it cut you off from something that might turn out great? Don't give your mom's bitterness or Carl's stupidity that much power over you. You're too smart for that."

"That's quite a speech from a guy spending Christmas at home with his dad."

His eyes widened. "That's a mean thing for such a fine Christian girl to say," he said.

"I'm tough," she said. "You haven't seen that side of me yet, that's all."

"I like it." He chuckled. "What else you got to show me?"

"You don't have the time," she said. "You're leaving the day after Christmas, remember?"

He smiled again, and she loved his dimples. "Are you saying you want me to stay longer?" he asked.

"I'm saying nothing of the sort."

"You wouldn't admit it if you were, would you?"

"Of course not."

"Why? What could it hurt?"

Jenna dropped her eyes. "It could hurt me," she said, the honesty pouring out before she could stop it.

"That's not my plan," he said.

She glanced back up. "What is your plan?"

He took a drink of water. "Not sure I have one," he finally said. "Got a lot on my mind."

"Tell me about that."

"I'm trying to make a decision," he said. "I've developed software to help clean up unwanted spam. A company wants to buy it. I have to give them an answer before Christmas."

"Not much time left."

"No, I'll call them in the morning."

"You know yet what you're going to do?"

He rubbed his eyes. "At first I didn't think I wanted to sell. But the last couple of days, I don't know. I've worked like a slave for years, and the idea of getting out of it free and clear, spending some time off, suddenly looks real attractive."

"Are you really a tycoon like Nelson said?" she asked. "Going to make millions from the sale of your intellectual property?"

"You looking for a man with money?"

"No, just curious."

Rem nodded. "I'll make a few dollars if I sell," he said. "But not that much; I've got some debts to pay."

"Too bad. I hoped you'd struck it rich."

"I can start over," he said. "I've done it before."

"I thought I'd ask you for money for Mickey," she said.

He sat up straighter. "You're serious, aren't you?"

"Maybe. I hadn't thought of it before, but why not? I've asked everybody else. You got some to give?"

He chuckled. "How's all that coming along?"

She dropped her head. "It's not," she admitted sadly. "I'm at a dead end. Timing is crucial in something like this. Mickey needs the transplant now, but we don't have the money to make it happen, plus we have to use what we've collected so far to pay the hospital here. Looks like it's over."

"So the kid dies?"

"I'm afraid so. Another wonderful success added to my resume. Seems I can't do anything right."

"You do lots of things right, a real Miss Do-Gooder."

"I wish you wouldn't say that," she said. "It sounds sarcastic."

"But aren't you? Have I got it wrong? I suspect you've been that way a long time, maybe since you were a child."

"You're the psychiatrist again?"

"You're avoiding the question."

She stared at him but she knew he'd hit a hot button. "Okay," she admitted. "I've always tried to fix things, to make people happy. And yes, I did that with my mom and dad, all through their lousy marriage. But I never get it right."

Rem leaned to her. "You try though," he said softly. "That's a good thing, not a bad one."

"I'd like to succeed every now and again though—like with Mickey."

Rem looked out the window. "I wish you could," he said. "It's not fair, letting a kid die because there's not enough money to pay some medical bills."

"He's got less than a 50 percent chance even with the transplant," Jenna said.

"He deserves the opportunity though," Rem said.

"Yes, but it's out of our hands now, up to the Lord."

Rem rubbed his eyes and looked at his plate, and she knew the mention of the Lord had bothered him. Unsure what to do, she picked up her fork but then laid it down again. "Tell me something," she said. "It's confused me since last night."

He nodded and she continued. "You told Nelson you didn't like preachers. Yet I know for a fact that your mom loved the Lord, the church, everything about it. What happened to you? Your dad too; I hardly ever see him in church. "

"It's a long story," he said. "Not sure I've got time before I take you home."

"My mom's probably got the cops looking for me already. A few more minutes won't hurt."

He rubbed his chin as if thinking about confiding in her but then shook his head. "Let's just say I had faith a long time ago," he said. "As much as anybody. But . . . well . . . things happened."

109

"What kinds of things?"

Sadness filled his eyes, and she wondered what lay behind it. She reached for his hands, but he pulled them away and put them in his pockets. "It's not worth talking about," he said.

"Maybe it is."

"Not tonight."

"Someday?"

"Maybe."

"I can tell it hurt you," she said.

"The Lord's got a lot of explaining to do someday," he said. "Leave it at that. And eat your steak."

Seeing he would say nothing else, she picked up her fork and started to work on the steak, but for the most part her appetite failed her. When they left about forty-five minutes later, neither she nor Rem had eaten much of anything. Rem drove her to her car at the day care center, both of them saying little. When he pulled to a stop, she reached quickly for the door handle, but he touched her back and she faced him.

"I'd like to see you again," he said. "Maybe tomorrow afternoon?"

"I don't know," she said. "Tomorrow is Christmas Eve day. It'll be so busy."

"Christmas day then?"

She shook her head. He wasn't a believer. No reason to let herself get interested in a man like Rem. "I have to see Mom, then Dad. We do it every year."

"Then when?" he asked.

She thought a second. "Come to Christmas Eve service tomorrow night," she suggested. "I'll sit with you after the choir sings."

"Not my idea of a date," he said. "And won't it ruin your reputation?"

"I'll just tell people I was trying to lead you to the Lord."

"I'm sure they'll believe you."

"So you'll come?"

"Let me think about it."

Her face lit up at the possibility, and she suddenly felt more hopeful than she had in a long time. Rem leaned closer, his eyes bright. She held her breath, not sure what to do.

"Is it okay if I kiss you?" he asked matter-of-factly.

"I don't know; I haven't kissed a man in a long time."

"It's like riding a bike. Once you've done it, you don't forget."

Confused, she dropped her eyes. She wanted to kiss him but saw no point in it. Why start up something that held no future? Yet what could a small Christmas flirtation hurt? She faced him again, her heart racing. "I've ridden a bike a few times," she said.

"You think you remember how?"

"Shut up and see," she said.

He kissed her, his lips soft. At first she stayed stiff, afraid. But he felt so strong and smelled so warm, like the fireplace at the restaurant. In spite of the warning bells in her head, she closed her eyes and relaxed into his arms. He touched her face, her hair and ears. His fingers were smooth and gentle. She shivered under them. He eased off the kiss and pulled back.

"You ride a bike real well," he whispered.

"Glad I haven't forgotten how," she murmured.

"Me too."

Silence fell on the car for several seconds. Jenna took a deep breath. "I expect I need to go now," she said.

"You sure?"

"No, but I think it's best. Come to church tomorrow, 11 p.m."

"I'll call and let you know."

"You'll be there."

"We'll see."

She left him, her heart pounding, her mind awhirl.

9

Rem woke the next morning to the sound of the William Tell Overture. Confused, he jumped up, looked around, then realized it was his cell phone. "Yeah," he mumbled as he answered.

"It's Lisa."

Boomer walked through his bedroom door and padded over to him.

"What time is it?" he yawned into the phone.

"After eight. You still asleep?"

Rem scratched Boomer's head. "What's going on?" he asked Lisa.

"You've got to come back to Atlanta," she said.

Rem plopped down on the bed. "Don't think so," he said. "I've made my decision."

"Good."

"Yeah, stayed up late last night thinking. I want to sell."

"Really?" She sounded surprised.

"Yeah, their offer made sense. It'll leave us about a million apiece, clean and clear. I need some time to clear my head, decide what I want to do when I grow up."

"I wish it was that simple," Lisa said. "But Stanfield called me this morning."

"So?" Rem wakened further.

"She's added a condition to the sale. Said when she got back to her office yesterday, her boss chewed her out, demanded this or the deal's off."

Rem walked to the window and gazed out. Gray clouds hung low, and frost covered the glass. It looked like snow might fall before night. Boomer nuzzled up to his knee. "What's the condition?" Rem asked.

"Stanfield says you've got to come with the deal—a three-year commitment. You stay on to manage the development of the software, clean up the last of the bugs, make sure it's ready for market."

Rem rubbed his eyes again. Stanfield's request made sense, but he knew without debate he didn't want to do it. He'd spent close to twelve hours a day almost every day since college dealing with computer software in one way or another, and the thought of continuing that for three more years set his teeth on edge. It might be okay if he was his own boss, but coming and going with somebody looking over his shoulder made his skin crawl. More than ever he realized he needed a change, something to refresh his body and soul, give him a chance to get a grip on his future.

"I can't do it," he told Lisa. "Tell Stanfield you'll take my place; you know as much about the program as I do."

"I don't think she'll like that."

"She's got no choice."

"But she does, and you and I both know it."

Rem chewed on a thumbnail for a second. This wasn't what he wanted to do today. "Let me think a minute," he said.

"Okay."

Rem carried the phone toward the kitchen, and Boomer followed him. Rem smelled bacon as he entered and saw Roscoe standing over a skillet full of bacon frying on the stove. He moved to his dad and peered over his shoulder. Roscoe turned and pointed a spatula at him but didn't speak. Rem walked to the window. The mountains loomed in the distance. "You sure Stanfield is set on seeing me today?" he asked Lisa.

"Dead sure."

"Okay," he said. "But she's going to hear the same thing I just told you. I'm going to sell but not stay on. I want some space from Atlanta for a while."

"Tell it to Stanfield."

"I think there's a ten o'clock flight. See you about noon."

"At the airport."

Rem hung up and looked at Boomer. "Weird," he said.

Boomer tilted his head as if to ask, "What?"

"I've decided to sell something I thought was more important than anything else, but I'm not sad at all."

Boomer smiled with pleasure.

"I'm the opposite of sad," Rem said. "I'm . . . I'm free . . ."

Boomer panted happily, and Rem faced his dad.

"I got to go to Atlanta," he said. "But I plan to come

115

back later today, maybe go to church tonight. You think I can hang around here for a few weeks after that, maybe longer?"

Roscoe faced him. "What's bringing you back here all of a sudden?"

"Maybe I want more time to share sterling conversation with you."

Roscoe faced the skillet again. "Yeah, I thought that was it."

Rem smiled and stepped to his dad. "You keep eating bacon like this and you'll be dead soon."

"Always the encourager, aren't you?"

Rem put a hand on his dad's shoulder, and Roscoe turned to him.

"I'm coming back," Rem said, seriously this time. "For a lot of reasons; spending some time with you is one of the biggest ones."

Roscoe arched an eyebrow. "You're acting weird today."

"Yeah, but good weird, don't you think?"

"Woman weird is what I think," Roscoe said. "You're sweet on Jenna Newsome, aren't you?"

Rem shook his head. "It's not that way."

"No," Roscoe said, facing his bacon again. "I'm sure it's not."

Rem smiled. He'd go to Atlanta one more time, then come back to Hilltop to figure out what he wanted to do next. Heck, he might stay here a long time. Who knew?

The morning passed like a pleasant blur for Jenna. She

awoke just past 7:30, a warm glow pulsing through her body from memories of last night. After eating a quick breakfast, she hurried out to finish some last-minute errands—a stop at the beauty shop to trim her hair and have her nails done; a trip to the grocery store for a few side dishes to go with the turkey she'd already bought; a run by the church to leave Nelson and Julie their Christmas present, a piece from the Dickens Christmas Village she knew they collected. Everything seemed to sparkle as she moved through her tiny town—the Christmas lights seemed brighter, the smell of the air crisper, the sound of the carols clearer. A wide smile stayed on her face all morning, and although she knew she shouldn't let herself get too carried away over a man as temporary as Rem, she wallowed happily in her emotions. She liked him, plain and simple, and felt confident he liked her. So what if he'd disappear in less than twenty-four hours? Atlanta wasn't that far away.

Finished with her errands, Jenna headed to her mom's to leave the groceries so Margaret could start preparing tomorrow's dinner. Although Jenna had offered for years to help with the cooking, her mom always refused.

"Christmas dinner is a mom's task," Margaret always asserted. "You bring the food, I'll cook it."

Her arms full of grocery sacks, Jenna pushed through the back door. "I'm here!" she yelled as she entered the kitchen. "Got the trimmings for the turkey!"

She placed the groceries on the table as her mom entered. "Hey, Mom," Jenna said brightly, moving to give Margaret a hug.

Her mom stopped before she reached her, her face as frozen as an ice sculpture. Jenna hugged her quickly,

117

but her mom didn't return the hug. Jenna stepped back, her nerves suddenly tight as she realized the problem. "Did Dad come by or something?" she asked.

"No," Margaret said.

"Then what's going on?"

Margaret wiped her hands on her apron and moved to the coffeepot on the stove. "Nothing," she said. "Don't worry about me."

Jenna sighed, weary from the drama in her mother's words. Although she had a suspicion about the cause of Margaret's attitude, she hoped she was wrong. Either way, she had to find out. She wanted things cleared up before Christmas.

"Have a seat," Jenna offered, pulling out a chair. "Tell me the problem."

Margaret brought her coffee and sat down. Jenna took a spot across from her. "We don't have time for our usual theatrics," Jenna started. "So go ahead and let me hear it."

"You think you're so smart, don't you?" Margaret started, her hands folded neatly in her lap.

"No, but I've got a lot to do and so do you. Christmas is tomorrow, and I don't want this hanging over us all day. So let's get this over with."

Margaret sipped her coffee as if having tea with the queen of England, then placed her cup in its saucer. "You were out late last night." She sniffed. "Past midnight; I know because I called you three times, the last time at twelve."

Jenna rubbed her eyes; just as she'd guessed. "I went to Asheville for dinner," she said. "Do you have a problem with that?"

"You went with Rem Lincoln, didn't you?"

"What if I did?" Jenna's face flushed with anger at having to explain. "Since when is it a crime to go to dinner with a man?"

Margaret sipped coffee again. "It's not a crime," she said. "But you have a reputation in this town, and so do I. Running around with a man like Lincoln will wreck your name."

Jenna balled her fists and stood, her eyes flashing heat. "I'm thirty years old!" she stammered, unwilling to placate her mom any longer. "I'd think you'd want me on a date, Rem Lincoln or not. What's wrong with what I did? Tell me that. Where's the harm, the sin?"

"No sin," Margaret said. "But I worried about you when I couldn't get you, especially so late."

Jenna sat back down, her blood steaming. She'd come to the end of her rope, and her mom might as well know it. Maybe it would ruin Christmas, but so what? She'd spent tons of time and energy in the last few years trying to please her mother yet had always come up short. Perhaps it was time to stand up to her.

"Look," she said, her hands flat on the table. "I've tried to honor you, listen to your advice. But where's it gotten me? Nowhere, that's where. I'm stuck in Hilltop—single, lonely, a failure. It's time that changed."

Her voice rose as she continued. "Yeah, Rem Lincoln is probably headed out of here in a day or so. Big deal. If he wants to see me again, I'm going to see him, either here or in Atlanta. Yes, maybe I'll even go down there, leave you here by yourself; I know that's a shocker. But I've got to start living my own life, stop trying to fix yours and Dad's. I've done that for a long time, but it's

119

got to stop. Can't you see that, for my sake and yours too? I've got to break this cycle, no matter how much it hurts, no matter how afraid I am of doing it."

Slightly unnerved that she'd spoken so angrily, she paused to take a breath and give her mom a chance to respond.

"That's a long speech," Margaret said, obviously untouched by it.

Jenna shook her head. Talking to her mom sometimes felt like hitting a stone wall with a feather.

"He had an affair, you know," Margaret said.

Jenna pulled back. "What?"

"An affair—your dad."

"I don't understand."

Margaret brushed back her hair with both hands. "When you were eleven. A woman at his office. It went on for close to three years before I caught them. She had written him a nice little love note; he brought it home in a suit pocket. I found it, took it to him. He admitted it once I showed him the note."

"Dad had an affair?" The meaning slowly settled on Jenna, and she stood and walked to the window.

"Yes, a dirty little secret I've kept from you."

Jenna's breath shortened as her heart sank.

"I stayed with him though," Margaret said. "Stayed right through it, tried to make the marriage work. Didn't want to destroy everything we'd built, our business, our friends. I thought we'd made it too; twelve years passed, and then he dared come and ask for a divorce. That's the most amazing part. The boldness of the man, asking for a divorce from me! I'll never forgive him for that."

Jenna faced her mom again as silence came to the

room. Disappointment in her dad quickly ran through her, and she wanted to feel angry with him but found it impossible. It had happened so long ago, what good would anger do now? Another question came to mind. What relevance did her dad's past transgression have to what she and her mom had been discussing? Confused, she walked back to her mom and stood over her. "Why didn't you tell me this a long time ago?" she asked.

"I didn't want to hurt you," Margaret said, reaching for her hand. "You were so young, so fragile. No girl needs to hear such a thing about her father; about men, the way they are, the way they'll hurt you."

"Then why are you telling me now?" Jenna asked.

Margaret pursed her lips. "You know why," she said.

Jenna's eyes steeled and she pulled away. "You're trying to manipulate me," she seethed. "Make me afraid of men, Rem or anybody else."

"No!" Margaret shouted, also standing now. "I'm trying to warn you! Keep you from making the same mistake I did. You've already suffered once; you know what a man can do to you—ruin your life!"

"You'd rather I let you ruin it!" Jenna argued. "Let you dictate what happens to me!"

"No!" Margaret countered. "I want you to find a husband if that's what you want, I really do. But not a Rem Lincoln. I know the type; so do you. He's probably got ten girlfriends, a different woman every night. He's just like your dad—busy, hurried, tied to his work, all charm and smile, sweet words and cute looks. But inside he's an empty shell. You know it as well as I do; he'll never be there when you need him, never support you like he should. And he's not even a believer. You know he's not good for you."

Jenna clenched her jaw to ward off her mom's words, but inwardly she also wondered if her mom had it right. Did Rem have scores of women? Would he hurt her? Did work keep him preoccupied? Would he ever claim any kind of faith?

In her confusion, another thought hit her. Had her mom made up this tale about her dad? Was that possible? Yes, she realized. Although she knew her mom loved her, she also suspected it wasn't beyond her to say such a thing if she thought it might bend Jenna to her will.

"I need to go," Jenna said suddenly. "I need time to consider all this."

Margaret touched her hand. "You do that," she said. "You'll realize I'm right."

Jenna turned to leave.

"I do love you," Margaret said.

Jenna paused once more and faced her mom. "I know you do," she said.

"I wouldn't say anything to your dad about what I told you," Margaret said softly.

"Why not?"

"Think about it," Margaret said. "You're the most important thing in his life, and he'd never want you disappointed in him. If he thought you knew this, that I'd told you, it would crush him and he'd come after me. It would make what little connection we have even worse, a lot more unpleasant. You don't want that, do you?"

Jenna rubbed her face and shook her head as she realized her mom had it all under control. She knew exactly what buttons to push to blackmail Jenna, to keep her from finding the truth.

Without another word, Jenna left the house. Climbing into her car, she hoped Rem would call before lunch. She really needed to talk to somebody, and he, an outsider to everyone she knew, seemed the only safe person to confide in.

Rem arrived at his office at about 1:30, Lisa at his side. Stanfield entered fifteen minutes later, alone this time but as punctual as ever, a tan suit covering her body, her hair pulled back in a way that made her cheekbones stand out. Rem admired the way Stanfield looked both tough and feminine at the same time, a difficult achievement for sure. Everybody took their places at the table in his small conference room, Stanfield across from him and Lisa. Rem held a bottle of water and offered Stanfield one, but she refused.

"It's the day before Christmas," Stanfield said firmly. "Let's do our business and get out of here."

Rem leaned forward. "Our business is already done," he said. "You made an offer; we accepted it. Then you put a new condition on it. I can't agree to that condition, so we revert to the original offer. We're ready to sell based on that agreement."

Stanfield scratched her earlobe. "I apologize for the added requirement," she said, her tone softer. "My supervisor added it when I carried back the papers. But I'm afraid it's nonnegotiable."

"Lisa is as knowledgeable as me," Rem said.

Stanfield nodded. "I'm sure that's true," she said. "But we want you; it's that simple. You come or the deal's off."

Rem sat back, his jaw firm. Stanfield seemed determined to push him into something he didn't want. Was she bluffing? His cell phone rang, and not wanting the distraction, he pulled it from his pocket and handed it to Lisa without checking the caller ID. Lisa stood, stepped out of the room, and answered the phone.

It surprised Jenna when a woman answered Rem's phone, and she momentarily lost her voice. Who was this, and why did she have Rem's phone?

"Yeah," she said after a couple of seconds. "I'm trying to reach Rem Lincoln. Is this his number?"

"It is, but he's not available. Can I take a message?"

Jenna started to ask the woman why she had Rem's phone but then realized it wasn't any of her business. She'd gone out with the man one time; what right did she have to ask anything? "No," she said. "No message."

"You sure?"

"Yes."

"Okay."

Jenna hung up and collapsed into a chair by her kitchen table. For reasons she couldn't explain, tears suddenly filled her eyes. She'd waited all morning for Rem to call, but when noon arrived and she hadn't heard from him, she'd done something she'd never have done even a week ago. She'd called his house. Roscoe had answered and told her Rem had gone back to Atlanta for some kind of year-end business deal. Disappointed, Jenna had started to hang up, but then Roscoe had offered her Rem's cell phone number and she'd taken it and written it down.

It had taken over an hour after she'd hung up to work up the courage to call the cell number. Was that too forward, pushy even? But who else could she tell what her mother had revealed? Nobody in Hilltop, that was for sure.

Her hands shaking, she'd punched in Rem's number. But what had it gotten her? Heartache, that's what. Rem obviously lived with a woman in Atlanta. Why else would a woman have his cell phone? Her mom was right; Rem probably had lots of women. It was crazy for her to get interested in him.

Jenna wiped her eyes, took a deep breath, and stood. All right, she'd made a mistake, but that was behind her and she wouldn't do it again. Rem Lincoln was history.

❧

Rem knew he had to make a decision but still didn't know which way to go. To his relief, Lisa walked back in, and he turned to her. She handed over his cell phone and sat down beside him.

"Time to choose," Rem said, pocketing the phone. "What'll it be?"

"Up to you," Lisa said.

Rem smiled and faced Stanfield again. "I've got a counterproposal," he told her. "What if we take . . . what if I take five hundred thousand less? You hire Lisa as your consultant for three years. If you still need me, I come on a year from now as her assistant. This is a win-win situation. You get the leadership you need from a cocreator of the program, and it costs you less money. If necessary, I can still become available—but not until, and not unless, I have to."

Stanfield's eyes widened as she considered the notion, but Lisa didn't like it. "I won't let you do this!" she whispered, leaning close to Rem. "After our debts are paid, you'll barely clear half a million, not nearly enough for all the work you've put in."

Rem held up a hand. "I'll clear enough," he whispered back. "My mind's set."

He faced Stanfield again as she pulled out a cell phone. "I need to check with my supervisor," she said. "But this sounds possible."

She stood and walked to the hallway.

Rem rose too and closed the door. Lisa looked at him as if he'd lost his mind. "I don't get it," she said. "You didn't even want to sell when you left here for Christmas. What's changed?"

He put his hands in his pockets. "I'm not sure," he said. "But it's just not that important to me anymore. The money, the frantic rush every day. I'm . . . I don't know . . . I've got some things going on right now."

"What's happened?" Lisa pressed. "Your dad okay?"

Rem nodded. "Ornery as ever, but his health is no worse, if that's what you mean. It's not him, I don't think."

"Then what?"

Rem propped a foot against the wall. "It's complicated," he said. "But . . . I don't know . . . I've run into some old friends back in Hilltop. There's this preacher. I went to State with him, and he's now a pastor back home."

"You're getting religion on me?"

"No, that's not it. But Nelson—that's his name—is a smart guy. Not one of these shout-until-your-head-falls-off kind of preachers, but intelligent, thoughtful. I'm interested in what he's got to say, that's all, like I'm interested in most everything else."

Lisa took off her glasses and placed them on the table. "There's nothing wrong with any of that," she said. "I know a lot of great people trying to find some kind of spirituality. But that's no reason to drop everything, all you've worked on, and head to the mountains. Why can't you do your searching right here?"

Rem glanced out at Stanfield, but she had her back to him, her cell phone still at her ear. "Who was on the phone a minute ago?" he asked.

"Don't know. Some woman."

Rem pulled out his cell phone, checked his call log, and recognized the area code but not the number. "A woman?"

"Yeah, she sounded surprised when I answered."

Rem punched the call return, and the number rang to an answering machine. Jenna's voice told him to leave a message.

"Who is she?" Lisa asked.

Rem smiled. "Another old friend I met in Hilltop."

Lisa tilted her head. "You're leaving Atlanta for a woman?"

Rem started to answer, but Stanfield turned his way and gave him a thumbs-up before he could. Lisa muttered something about not believing what she'd just heard, but Rem ignored her and opened the door for Stanfield.

Stanfield strutted back in, and they started talking about the terms of their deal. Less than an hour later, she left the room.

Rem told Lisa he'd answer all her questions in due time, then sent her home and took a taxi to the airport. Although he'd just signed an agreement to sell something at a lot cheaper price than he'd ever imagined, he still felt at ease. For the first time in years, he had something he'd long missed . . . some free time. The question was, what was he going to do now that he owned it? Was Lisa right? Was he doing all this for a woman? Or was something else behind it, something even more important?

As his plane took off for Asheville, Rem's mind clouded more and more with confusion. Somehow, though, he knew that the next couple of days would tell him a lot, perhaps more than he ever wanted to know.

∞10∞

Rem tried all afternoon to reach Jenna but with no success. As soon as he landed in Asheville, he called again, leaving his name and number on her answering machine a couple more times, but she didn't call back. By the time he'd returned to Hilltop, night had long since fallen and he'd become more and more confused. Jenna had called him; what did she want and why hadn't she called him back?

He drove by her apartment as soon as he entered town but didn't find her. Frustrated, he tried to guess where she was—her mom's house maybe? He piloted his Lexus in that direction, and Margaret met him at the door when he arrived, her hair neatly pressed, her eyes suspicious.

"I'm Rem Lincoln," he said, still on the porch because Margaret hadn't invited him inside. "Is Jenna here?"

Margaret shook her head, and Rem waited for some explanation, but she offered none.

"Do you know where I can find her?" he asked, exasperation in his voice.

"Why don't you leave her alone?" Margaret said.

Rem stepped back half a pace and wondered what the woman had against him. "Is there a problem I should know about?" he asked.

Margaret sniffed the air as if walking past a garbage dump in July. "Jenna is happy," she said. "She doesn't need to get hurt again."

Rem struggled to stay calm. Although he had no clue why, Margaret obviously thought poorly of him. "Look," he said, "I'm a friend of Jenna's and have no plans to hurt her or anyone else. I just wanted to see her a few minutes. She called me earlier today; I tried to call her back but couldn't reach her. Do you have any idea where she is?"

"If she didn't call you back, maybe it's because she doesn't want to talk to you."

Rem became even more frustrated. "Do you know for a fact she doesn't want to talk to me?"

Margaret's eyes narrowed, and he saw genuine anger in them and wondered why she hated men so much. "No," she finally admitted. "I don't know it for sure, but I feel confident I'm right."

"So you won't tell me where I can find her?"

"I have no intention of doing such a thing."

His fists clenched, Rem nodded as politely as he could manage, then stalked off the porch. Back in his car, he tried to figure out what to do. Should he go back to Jenna's apartment and wait? But if he did that and she really didn't want to see him, she'd get awfully upset, and he didn't want that. Then where could he find her?

The grocery store? He headed the Lexus that way but

saw as he drove up that it was closed. Where next? The hospital! Perhaps she'd gone to visit with the Stracks.

Knowing no other place to try, Rem headed to the hospital. One way or another he planned to find Jenna. If she didn't want to see him, fine. If he'd scared her off last night, okay. But he wanted her to say that to his face. If she did, he'd leave her absolutely alone. Just make it plain, that's all he wanted.

Jenna's eyes widened as she walked into Mickey Strack's hospital room and saw Rem standing with Brenda and Tom beside the baby's bed. Brenda stepped to her and smiled thinly, and Jenna gave her a quick hug. Rem glanced at his shoes, then back at Jenna. His eyes looked moist, and she wondered why.

"I came here looking for you," he explained. "Met Tom and Brenda here, Mickey too." He pointed to the sleeping baby. A plastic bubble covered Mickey's bed to protect him from infections.

Jenna's heart hardened for reasons she couldn't explain, and her anger quickly rose. Rem had no business here! She glanced at Brenda and Tom; both looked pale in the room's dim light.

"They're sending Mickey home in less than an hour," Tom said. "They've done all they can."

Jenna's heart shriveled, and the sense of failure she'd worn the last day or so hit hard again. Although free of disease at the moment, Mickey would certainly catch something in the next few weeks, and that would be the end, and she could do nothing to stop it. She wondered if she looked as worn out as Brenda.

"It ought to be a crime," Rem said, his hands in his pockets. "Treating a kid this way, turning him out without the treatment he needs."

Jenna heard sincerity in Rem's words, and she liked that. And he had so many other great qualities too, but she knew she couldn't listen to him, couldn't let herself feel anything but cold. Rem deserved none of her affection. He had a woman in Atlanta. She squared her shoulders and decided to send him on his way.

"Excuse us a minute," she said to Tom and Brenda. They nodded, and she took Rem's arm and steered him from the room. In the hallway, she faced him, her face tight. "What are you doing here?" she asked.

"I tried to call you back," he said. "I left three or four messages; didn't you get them?"

"I got them."

"Then why didn't you call me again?"

"I didn't see the point," she said, deciding to leave out the part about his girlfriend answering the phone. "You're leaving tomorrow; we both know it."

He shook his head. "I don't get it," he said. "Last night you didn't seem worried about when I'd leave. You seemed fine to let things happen nice and easy like. But now you're like a different person; you call me but then won't take my calls when I call back. That's crazy!"

"Maybe to you," she said, "but not to me."

"What happened?" he said. "You owe me an explanation."

"I don't owe you anything! We went to dinner, that's it. Both of us got a little romantic on a cold winter night before Christmas. We kissed. So what? Let's not make too much out of it."

Rem shoved his hands into his pockets. "I'm trying to figure this out," he said. "You called me during a meeting. Lisa answered the phone, but you wouldn't give her a name or number." He paused and stared at his shoes. Suddenly he glanced back up. "That's it!" he sputtered. "Lisa answered my phone. You think she's a live-in or something!"

He waited for a response, but Jenna kept quiet. No reason to argue with him, she figured. He could lie as easily as the next man. Her mother knew about that; now she did too.

Rem reached for her hands, but she pulled away. "Just go," she said. "That's the best thing; we're too different."

"But Lisa's my business partner," he explained. "She's married to a guy big enough to crush my skull with one hand. I can prove it to you. Here, let's call her."

He pulled out his phone, and Jenna again saw his sincerity and wanted to believe him but knew that even if she did, it wouldn't matter. She didn't want to get hurt again, and Rem possessed every trait she'd ever feared in a man—he attracted women too easily and worked too hard and didn't have a religious bone in his body. She might as well end this before it ever got started. She touched his forearm, her anger gone but her resolve still set.

"Go on home," she said gently. "Let it go."

He hesitated, the phone in hand. "You're not going to give me a chance, are you?" he asked.

She slowly shook her head.

133

"You're judging me," he said. "Without any cause and without listening, you're making decisions based on what somebody else did to you, Carl who left you at the altar, your mother's advice, maybe a whole lot of other things I don't even know about. But you've been hurt, and I'm being judged for it."

"Maybe so," she finally managed. "But I can't help it."

"It's not too Christian though, is it?"

"What?" She looked at him, her heart grieved at what he'd suggested.

"You claim you're a Christian," he said, "but you're not judging me for myself. That's not right, is it?"

"I don't know," she said.

"Okay." He pulled his arm away and stood up straight. "I'm leaving now," he said. "I won't bother you anymore. But you need to know I'm not a bad man. Too bad you'll never find that out for yourself."

She nodded. "Maybe I'll run into you," she said. "We can be friends."

"I expect not," he said. "I'll leave tomorrow."

She sighed. "Take care," she said.

"What's it to you?" he asked.

Tears moistened her eyes, but she brushed them away. She didn't want to hurt him, but better him than her.

He faced her one more time, and the pain in his eyes seemed so familiar. She'd seen that pain before, somewhere . . . but where? She wanted to scream and make the memory come back. He'd said they'd met before high school, and she felt sure they had. He wasn't lying about that, but she couldn't push the moment to her consciousness.

"I'm sorry about the kid," he said, breaking her thoughts. "I know you tried hard."

"Everybody did," she said, glad he hadn't left yet. "But I guess it just wasn't the Lord's will."

He stuck his hands in his pockets again. "The Lord's will," he said. "You think you know what that is?"

"No," she said. "I don't guess I do."

"Let me know if you find it," he said.

"I'll do that."

He leaned close, kissed her on the forehead, and then turned and walked away. Watching him leave, she got the distinct sense that she'd just made a terrible mistake. But given what she knew at the moment, what else could she do but let him go?

⚜

Although Rem spent the next couple of hours helping Roscoe put up a Christmas tree and hang a couple of stockings, his temper got worse and worse. By the time Roscoe hung the star on top and they sat down for a cup of coffee and a piece of fudge, his anger had risen hot enough to boil eggs. How dare Jenna judge him? She didn't know him, didn't know what he'd faced, what he'd endured. If she represented what it meant to be a Christian, then he had all the more reason to reject it.

"It's close to ten," Roscoe said, taking a bite of his last piece of fudge. "You mentioned this morning you might go to church; time to get ready if you are."

"You going?" Rem asked.

135

"Reckon not," Roscoe said. "Got me a bad head cold; don't want to spread it."

"Mama would want you there."

"I know, and I usually go on Christmas. Just can't make it this time."

Rem sipped his coffee. "How'd she do it, Pop? Hold her faith when . . . well . . . you know."

Roscoe licked his fingers. "Your mama kept it simple," he said. "Figured the Lord didn't promise us a rose garden; if life came up a stinker every now and again, well . . . what else should we expect?"

Rem wrapped both hands around his cup and tried to feel better. After his visit with Jenna, his spirits felt like somebody had mopped up a floor with them. All of a sudden he wanted to get out of Hilltop and put this awful episode behind him. If it wasn't too late, he might just call Stanfield the day after Christmas and see if he could still come on as a consultant with her firm. No extra charge.

"I told you I might hang around for a while," he told Roscoe. "But I've changed my mind. Fact is, I might head on back to Atlanta tonight."

"Tonight?" Roscoe looked stunned.

Rem sighed. "I don't know, just feeling restless all of a sudden."

"You beat all, boy."

"What?"

Roscoe picked up the last of Rem's fudge and popped it into his mouth. "You and Jenna Newsome already having troubles?"

"She's not for me," Rem said. "She's made that plenty plain. She's too pure for my kind."

"What kind is that?"

"You'd have to ask her; she seems to know it all."

"So you're going to run away," Roscoe said. "Let the first sign of trouble push you out of here with your tail tucked between your legs."

"You got a better idea?"

Roscoe eyed him as if studying a space alien. "Of course I do," he finally said. "You stay here and show her she's got you wrong, prove to her what kind of guy you are. You got to remember, that guy in Winston-Salem cut her deep. Plus, she's got a mama with an attitude so bitter it'd cut paint if you added water to it. No wonder she's a touch skittish, fearful. That's why she's judging you so hard; she's looking at you through eyes that have cried a lot of tears."

"Since when do you know so much about women?"

Roscoe smiled. "How you think I kept your mama happy all those years?"

"I thought it was your good looks and boyish charm."

"You can change her mind about you," Roscoe said. "I know what kind of guy you are; she just needs to know what I know."

Rem shook his head. "I'm not sure," he said. "She seems set in her ways. I'd have to 'get saved' or something to change her mind."

Roscoe washed down the fudge with the last of his coffee. "You might be right," he said. "But I wish you'd stay on at least until morning. Weatherman says we might get a few inches of snow tonight. Dangerous on the roads if that happens."

Rem hung his head, unsure what to do.

"We haven't exchanged gifts," Roscoe said. "You got to stay at least until then."

Rem nodded. "Let's do that now," he said. "Then I'll see."

"Okay, give me ten minutes. I got to wrap yours."

"Glad to see you're prepared."

Roscoe grinned, then stood and shuffled toward his room. Rem finished his coffee and studied his options. He wanted to stay, but he also wanted to leave. He considered what his dad had said, how he could stay and show Jenna his true character. But how? She didn't seem easily impressed, and he had no plan to pretend to believe something he didn't. If her big hang-up was his lack of faith, then he had nothing to offer her.

Standing, he headed to his room to get his things together. After he and his dad exchanged gifts, he'd leave town, no doubt about it.

⁂

Although Jenna usually arrived at church for Christmas Eve services about thirty minutes early to sing in the choir, she just couldn't manage it this time. If she'd had her way about it, she might not have gone at all. But not wanting to disappoint Nelson and Julie, not to mention her mom, she bundled up against the cold and sped through town just in time to put on her choir robe and take her place in the front row with the sopranos as the service started. Although she sang loudly as the hymns began, her heart felt as heavy as an iron and her eyes kept watering. The sense that she'd messed up badly kept rolling through her heart, and she wanted to do something about it but didn't know what. Rem would leave in the morning, and she'd probably never see him again.

Nelson welcomed the congregation and gave the children's sermon. The choir stood to sing the Christmas anthem they'd worked on for the last month. Jenna looked out at the congregation as she sang and tried to cheer up. The people she knew best and loved most sat in the pews before her. Green garlands decorated the balcony that hung over the back fourth of the church, and a tree decorated with Christian symbols stood to her right. Shoe boxes full of toys and clothes for needy children sat under the tree. The people wore green and red sweaters and vests and coats, and a soft golden glow oozed down from the chandelier that hung like a giant ornament from the center of the sanctuary ceiling. The choir finished singing and sat down. Nelson stood to offer his sermon, a shorter one tonight because they'd do the Lord's Supper when he finished, then light candles as everybody sang "Silent Night."

Jenna caught her mom's eye as Nelson started to preach and gave her as good a smile as she could muster. Her dad sat beside her mom, and she wondered if he had really had an affair. What if he had? Did she love him any less because of it? And what if he hadn't? What if her mom had lied about it? How would she feel about her mom? Disappointed yes, angry certainly. But would she stop loving her mom because of the lie?

Nelson chose an unusual text for a Christmas Eve sermon—the story of King Herod killing all the babies less than two years of age in his effort to snuff out the life of the baby Jesus. Nelson warmed quickly to his message, his voice rising with emphasis as he plowed into it.

"The mothers of Israel wept. They wept over the babies whose lives ended at the hands of Herod."

Jenna sat up straighter as Nelson's voice picked up even more steam. Where was he going with this message?

"I'm sure the mothers wondered, the fathers too. They wondered why God didn't put an end to Herod's terrible deeds. They wondered why God gave evil such a free rein. They wondered why God allowed death to snatch away from them the one thing they loved the most, the child they had birthed together."

Nelson's voice softened now, and the congregation sat on the edge of their seats. "We all have questions like that from time to time," Nelson said. "When a car crash kills a teenager, when a heart attack takes a granddad, when our company lays us off, when we study hard but still fail our geometry exam."

The congregation laughed a little and the tension eased a moment, but Nelson didn't let them rest long.

"I've asked these questions recently," Nelson admitted. "When I heard about little Mickey Strack. I'm not the only one either; I know that. You've wondered too. I know that Tom and Brenda have wondered," he said softly, nodding to the second pew where they sat with their daughter, Tess. "They've wondered why God allows such sickness in the life of a little boy like Mickey. They've cried out to God as these parents of Israel did. They've cried out because they've done everything they could but they've come up empty. They've not man-

140

aged to find enough money to pay for the treatment Mickey needs.

"It's enough to make you cry this Christmas," he whispered. "We've all done all we can. Many of you have given sacrificially. I know because I've seen you do it. Jenna Newsome did more than anybody. I know Jenna's got some questions and she's cried some tears." He turned and faced her, and she wiped her eyes as his words hit home. She had questioned, she realized, though she'd not admitted it to anyone.

"We all hear the weeping of Israel this Christmas Eve," Nelson said. "They cried and lamented because God let death loose on this Christmas night when Jesus breathed his first breath."

Jenna lifted her eyes past Nelson and tried to distance herself from his preaching. It was too sad for a Christmas message, and she didn't want to hear it. She wanted soft sentiment on Christmas Eve, something easy on the ears, something soothing to the heart. Why had Nelson chosen this message? Was it because of Mickey Strack? Did he believe the people needed to deal with this right now?

She looked into the balcony, trying to find a face to cheer her up. She spotted Handy and his wife, Martha, perched on the aisle of the next to last row, their usual spot. Her eyes moved past them, then widened as she saw Rem behind them, wearing a tan sport coat covering a black crew-neck sweater.

Jenna sat up straighter. How long had Rem been there? She glanced at Nelson. Did he know Rem had come?

Nelson moved ahead with his sermon. Jenna looked

141

back at Rem and wondered what he thought of Nelson's words.

"I wish I could tell you why God allowed this to happen this way. But I can't. Sometimes all we get is a mystery."

He looked at the congregation as if expecting them to give him an answer. When they didn't, he moved on. "I can say that because from the moment Jesus lay his little head down in that manger, God knew he'd one day lay his head down on the scratchy bark of a cross. God would one day weep just as these families of Israel wept. That's the whole meaning of the incarnation. God identified with us in every way. In Jesus, God suffered and knew the salty taste of tears."

Jenna watched Rem as Nelson preached, and it surprised her when she saw him wipe his eyes with the back of his hand. Had Nelson's words touched him enough to make him cry? But why? What about Nelson's message would make any difference to Rem? He'd made plain his indifference, if not his antagonism, toward anything religious.

Nelson's voice picked up pace, and Jenna knew from past experience that he was moving toward the climax of his message.

"All of us feel pain!" he proclaimed. "Even God! But that's when the true test of faith comes. The true test of faith comes not when the sun shines and the sky stays blue but when the storms blow.

"The true test of faith comes not when the girl says yes to our invitation to the prom but when she laughs and says no.

"The true test of faith comes not when the baby

grows up big and strong but when the baby needs an operation and we can't find the money to pay for it.

"That's the true test of faith tonight as we celebrate the Christ child."

Nelson slowed now, and Jenna saw Rem slowly stand and move to the back wall. She wanted to run from the choir and go to him, but sitting on the front row, she knew she didn't dare.

"I know this isn't sweet to hear tonight," Nelson concluded, "but I believe we need to hear this message. When bad things happen to us—and if we live long enough, we can surely expect them to come—it's easy to become bitter and angry. It's easy to give up on God. But if we do that, we have to wonder if we really ever had any faith at all."

He stopped and looked at his congregation. "So here's the conclusion of what I want to say. God stands with us in our suffering. And even if we've left God because of it, God hasn't left us. God waits for us to come home, to give up our bitterness and turn back. That's what God offers, not an absence of pain but the promise of grace and forgiveness. Let's pray."

Everybody but Jenna bowed and closed their eyes. She kept hers on Rem. As Nelson began to pray, Rem ducked out of the balcony. Without thinking, Jenna stood, rushed out of the choir loft, and walked out a side door. In less than a minute, she reached the narthex, her choir robe flapping at her ankles. To her surprise, she heard somebody behind her and turned quickly and saw Julie headed her way, a hymnbook in hand.

"What are you doing?" Jenna whispered.

143

"You ran out of the choir. I figured something was wrong."

"Rem was here," Jenna panted, pushing open the front door and stepping into the cold. "He just left."

"I saw him earlier," Julie said, right behind her.

"You did?"

"Yeah, he came by the church before the service, wanted to talk to Nelson a few minutes."

The taillights of a car blinked at the edge of the parking lot, then sped away. Jenna's heart sank as she realized she'd missed him. She faced Julie. "I blew it," she said. "He came to the hospital to find me, but I treated him like dirt."

"He's leaving tonight," Julie said. "He told Nelson he'd call him later from Atlanta."

Jenna moved back to the church steps and sat down. Julie took a spot by her. A cold wind nipped at their cheeks.

"Did he say anything about me to Nelson?" Jenna asked quietly.

"He wanted us to give you this." Julie took an envelope from her hymnal and handed it to Jenna.

"What is it?"

"Why don't you open it and see?"

Her fingers trembling, Jenna tore open the envelope. Inside, she found a handwritten letter.

> Dear Jenna,
> Although you've already made up your mind about me, I want you to know that a long time ago I believed as deeply as you. But things happened.

One of these days I hope you'll remember where we met. If you do, you'll remember one of those things. Then you'll understand, at least that's my hope.

I also hope you'll find what you're looking for someday, something to bring you some happiness. Right now, I don't think you have much. Maybe that's judgmental, but that's the way I see it.

From time to time, I'll come back to Hilltop, and I'm sure we'll run into each other. When that happens, I want you to remember me fondly, the night we . . . rode a bike together.

Take care,

Rem Lincoln

Jenna's tears dripped on the letter. "I'm horrible," she sobbed. "He says we met years ago, but I can't remember it."

"What?" Julie asked.

"Here." She handed Julie the letter. "I have to find him before he leaves. I have to find out where we met, why that's so important. I have to ask him to forgive me. If he leaves before I do that, I don't know what I'll do."

"Try his house," Julie said.

"You think he's there?"

"I have no way of knowing, but you can try."

Jenna nodded, quickly hugged Julie, and ran toward her car, taking off her robe as she climbed in.

It took her less than ten minutes to reach Rem's house. To her sorrow, she saw no sign of his Lexus, but hoping maybe he'd parked in the garage, she hopped out anyway and sprinted to his front door. A light burned in the front window. She knocked hard.

"Hang on," she heard Roscoe yell a few seconds later.

She tried to calm down as she waited. What if Rem had already left?

The door opened, and Roscoe stood behind the screen door, a flannel shirt stretched over his full stomach, a tissue in hand.

"Miss Newsome," he said, obviously surprised. "It's a little late to be knocking on doors, don't you think?"

"I'm looking for Rem," she said quickly.

"He's already gone. You try his cell phone?"

"Yeah, on the way over. He didn't answer."

Roscoe shook his head. "He's a mite mixed up," he said. "Lots going on in his head right now. You're partly to blame for that."

Jenna glanced down, her spirits heavy. She started to leave but then hesitated. "Mr. Lincoln?"

"Yeah?"

"Can I ask you a question?"

"If you're not that particular about the answer."

She smiled. "Rem told me that he and I met somewhere years ago. I thought for a while maybe it was a line, but now I believe him. I've squeezed my brain every

146

way I can but haven't come up with when that happened. He ever talk to you about anything like that?"

Roscoe's brow wrinkled. "Not that I can recall," he said. "But truth is, we don't talk a whole lot. I'm not exactly Dr. Phil when it comes to listening."

She smiled again, recognizing where Rem got his sense of humor, but her grief made the smile brief. "I guess I'll try to reach him later," she said. "Once he's back in Atlanta. Merry Christmas." She turned to leave.

"We did come to Hilltop that one time though," Roscoe said. "You think it's possible you met Rem then?"

She faced him quickly. "When was that?"

He wiped his nose. "The year Rem turned eight."

"Why were you here?"

Roscoe pushed open the screen door. "Let me show you something," he said. "Maybe it'll explain a few things."

She followed him to the den. A fire burned in the fireplace. A deer head hung over the mantel. A brown leather sofa with a remote control in the middle sat in front of the television. Roscoe moved to the mantel, picked a picture off it, and handed it to her. She almost collapsed as she saw the picture and the memory rolled back up. How could she have forgotten? For the second time that night, tears flooded her eyes.

"It's so sad," she said.

Roscoe wiped his nose, and this time it wasn't because he had a cold. "Those were hard days," he said. "For all of us."

She took his hand. "Mrs. Lincoln never said anything," she said. "All the time I knew her from church."

"We agreed not to talk of it," he said. "Maybe that was a mistake."

She put the picture back on the mantel and faced Roscoe again. "I better go," she said. "If you talk to Rem tomorrow, please tell him I came by. Tell him I understand now."

Roscoe dropped his eyes. "I'm not supposed to tell you this," he said. "But I don't care what he does to me; I'm going to say it anyway."

"What?"

He looked up again. "He's not gone to Atlanta yet—but you didn't hear that from me."

"Where is he?"

"Where he always goes on the way out of Hilltop."

Jenna waited for him to explain, but when he didn't she suddenly understood his meaning. She'd find Rem where she'd first met him so long ago.

"He won't stay there long," Roscoe said. "Best you go if you plan to catch him."

Jenna quickly hugged Roscoe, then stepped back. "Will he forgive me?" she asked.

"As pretty as you are, I think there's a good chance of it."

She smiled and rushed out, her heart soaring. If Rem would forgive her, who knew what could happen then? After forgiveness, anything was possible.

∞11∞

Jenna saw Rem's Lexus as she turned into the cemetery, its silver paint glinting under the lights of her Bronco. Stepping quietly but quickly out, she trained a flashlight straight ahead and saw Rem standing hatless beside a small tombstone, his back to her. Without a word, she slipped over the grass toward him. A light smattering of snow began to show in her flashlight beam. She checked her watch—almost midnight.

She stopped about twenty feet from Rem and hoped he'd turn around, but he didn't. He kept his head down, his hands in his pockets. For the twentieth time since she'd left Roscoe's house, she rehearsed in her head what she wanted to say. But right now it all seemed lame, frail words that couldn't ever make up for the harsh way she'd treated him. When she opened her mouth, none of her planned words came out.

"Can I talk to you a second?" she asked quietly, raising the flashlight so she could see him better.

"I'd rather be alone," he said, his voice as cold as the air.

She waited another few seconds and prayed he'd give her a chance to explain. "I remember when we met," she offered.

"Dad tell you where to find me?" He still faced the tombstone. Her light lit up his back. Snowflakes danced lightly as they fell to the ground.

"Yes," she said.

"I'm sure you had to torture him to get him to talk."

She tried to determine if she heard any humor in his words but couldn't tell. "He showed me a picture," she said.

"That's how you remembered," Rem said. "He made it easy on you." He sounded resentful.

"I'm sorry I didn't remember sooner," she said. "But it was a long time ago."

"I suppose what changes one person's life forever isn't always memorable for everybody else."

"It's sad it's that way, but I think you're right. One person's tragedy is another person's passing event."

He nodded but didn't speak. She gathered her courage and took a step closer. He held up a hand but still didn't face her.

"I didn't invite you here," he said.

"I know, and I don't want to intrude."

"Then why are you?"

She bit her lip to hold back her tears. "I judged you," she offered. "I saw you through my own stupid problems. That wasn't fair. I see that now."

"Is that an apology?"

"Yes."

He shoved his hands into his pockets and turned to

face her. "I don't know that it matters now," he said. "But I accept it."

She tried to gauge his sincerity. Was he just letting her off the hook so he could leave without any more bother?

"Thanks for coming," he said. "At least we can part as friends."

She glanced up into the falling snow and tried to decide what to do, what to say. Was this it? A last few seconds together in a cemetery, then separated again forever? But why did she care? She didn't love him. How could she? They'd spent so little time together. Plus, he worked too much and seemed too flippant about a lot of things she cared most deeply about. Yet . . . she couldn't just let him go; something about him magnetized her, pulled her to him.

She focused on him again, studying his eyes in the flashlight's beam. His eyes looked back with a quiet strength. How could she ever have forgotten those eyes, the deep brown, the power in spite of the hurt, the depth that had obviously looked into places she'd never even considered? She couldn't let him go, not yet, not until she'd said all she'd come here to say.

"Your brother," she started, stepping another pace closer. "I saw him in the picture."

"We don't talk of my brother," he said.

"But maybe you should," she blurted. "Maybe it would help you . . . help you . . . I don't know . . . deal with it."

"It's not your place to say that," he said. "We deal with things as we do; nobody to interfere, nobody to say there's a right way or a wrong way."

151

"You're right," she said. "But I do want you to know I remember; and your dad didn't tell me any of this. Your brother died, and your family came to your dad's old hometown to bury him. I expect that's why your dad wanted to move here after he quit the police force."

"It's why I didn't want to move here," he said.

"I can understand that."

He took his hands from his pockets and balled them into fists at his side.

"Hilltop folks came to the funeral," she said. "Even though most of us didn't know your mom and dad, we knew your dad's folks."

"People brought casseroles," Rem said.

"Up here on the mountain, they always do."

Rem faced the tombstone again, and she moved slowly to his side. To her relief, he let her stay there. His hands relaxed a little.

"You sat down by this tombstone after the minister finished the service," she whispered. "On a day as bright as any I've ever seen. Everybody started talking. I sat down by you and asked your name."

"You weren't shy back then," Rem said.

"A man hadn't cut my heart out back then," Jenna said.

The snow thickened. "You asked me what happened," Rem said. "I told you. You asked my brother's name."

"Tyler," she said. "A good name. I liked it."

Rem wiped his eyes, then touched the top of the tombstone. "He died of leukemia," he said. "Not exactly the same as Mickey Strack's, but close enough. That's why this trip home has seemed so strange to me, ever since I saw you at the grocery store and heard about

152

Mickey. It was almost like reliving what happened to Tyler all those years ago."

"I'm sorry," Jenna said. "I had no idea."

"How could you? I didn't exactly let on about any of it."

They stood quietly as the snow fell. Jenna trained her flashlight on the tombstone.

"Robert Tyler Lincoln. 1979–1982. A child of the Lord."

Rem sat down on the ground and stared at the tombstone. Without asking permission, Jenna sat beside him and tried to take his hand, but he pulled it away and shoved it into his jacket.

"Is this why you lost your faith?" she asked, pointing the light at Tyler's name. "Your brother's death?"

"Not exactly."

"What then?"

He looked up. Snow fell into his face, but he didn't seem to notice. "A preacher," he said. "A young guy, the pastor of our church back in Knoxville. We prayed for Tyler, me and my mom and dad. The pastor said if we prayed and had faith, the Lord would heal Tyler. We prayed like you wouldn't believe, every night, every morning, all day long. My mom went on fasts, didn't eat for days while she prayed. But nothing happened. Tyler got worse; we prayed more. Tyler suffered, hurt, cried. Finally he died."

"You thought God let you down."

He shook his head. "No, we never doubted God, not really. But that preacher, he . . . ." Rem wiped his eyes again.

"What?" she asked. "Tell me."

He shook his head again. She reached for his hand once more, but again he refused to let her take it. "You have to say it," she said. "What did he do?"

Rem faced her. "He came to our house after the funeral," he said through gritted teeth. "He talked with my mom and dad; I sat on the floor and listened. Mom asked him why our prayers hadn't worked. The preacher took a big drink of tea and shrugged his shoulders like he was talking about the price of apples. Then he said that one of two things must have happened; either we didn't have enough faith or we had some hidden sin in our lives."

Jenna froze, her body numbed by the misguided words the minister had spoken. How could anybody, no matter how young and inexperienced, have said such things? Didn't he know the power such statements held, the power to alter a life the second the words came out?

"His words burned into my brain," Rem said. "Made me furious. Yeah, maybe I didn't have enough faith, maybe I had sin in my life. But my mom, my dad? They were as good as anybody, Mama especially. I decided then and there that the preacher didn't have a clue. Nobody could say that about my mom. I swore off preachers that day and the rest of religion not too long afterward and haven't seen much reason to ever change my mind."

"He was one bad apple," she said. "Nelson isn't that way."

"I know, but that doesn't fix what the guy in Knoxville did."

Snowflakes fell on Jenna's nose, and she brushed them off. "So what now?" she asked.

"What do you mean?"

"Do you plan on staying angry the rest of your life?"

"I don't know; I'm just taking it a day at a time."

"What about us?"

He wiped snow off his face. "I'm not what you need," he said. "You've made that plain."

"I don't know what I need," she said. "So how can you?"

"I'm not sure I'll ever trust a pastor again," he said. "The church either."

"I'm not asking you to change anything," she said. "That's between you and God."

"You think I need changing?"

She shivered as the snow began to fall faster. "We all need changing," she said.

"You think you do?" he asked, facing her.

"Sure."

"How so?"

"I'm too self-righteous, too judgmental. You've already told me that."

"And me?"

"Well, you need to give up your anger, bitterness. It'll eat you up if you let it; believe me, I know."

"Are you saying you've given yours up?"

She shook her head. "No," she said. "But I've decided to try. You can too."

The snow swirled around them, and the wind picked up. "You're going to freeze out here," he said.

"You could put your arm around me," she said.

He turned to her, surprise in his face. "You're awfully bold all of a sudden," he said.

"I'm turning into a popsicle," she said. "That'll make a girl bold."

He looked sideways at her. "What do you want from me?" he finally asked.

"Besides your jacket?"

"Yeah, other than that."

She reached for his hand one more time, and this time he let her take it. "I want you to stay in Hilltop a little longer," she said. "See what happens."

"You really think there's a chance for us?"

She squeezed his hand. "I'm not asking you to marry me," she said. "Just for us to spend a little time together. Maybe we can help each other—both of us have some things to get over. You keep me straight on my self-righteousness thing; I'll show you that not every preacher is like that guy in Knoxville."

"I can get Nelson to do that," he said.

She pinched his hand. "You're not making this easy," she said.

He became serious again. "Sorry," he said. "Guess I'm just a little scared."

"Of what?"

"I've carried my anger a long time; I don't know who I'll be without it."

"You might feel a whole lot freer. You ever think of that?"

"Yes, a lot."

"Then you'll stay?"

He sat quietly for at least a minute. The snow began to gather around their knees. Jenna shivered and her teeth chattered. Rem stood and pulled her up, and she wondered if she'd scared him off. He put both hands in his pants pockets. Her heart sagged again.

"You okay?" she asked.

He stared up into the falling snow as if to see some message in it. "I'm not sure what happens now," he said.

Jenna weighed what to do next. Should she press him further or give him space? Something told her she'd done all she could. She stepped back a half pace.

"I want you to stay here," she said more calmly than she felt. "But it's up to you now. Before we go our separate ways though, I feel like I have to say this. You're at a crossroads—no, not about me, but about yourself. I think . . . really I believe . . . that God brought you home this year to make you take a hard look at your life. Mickey Strack's situation opened up a vault you've kept locked a long time. Some bad things walked out of that vault, and they scared you. Still do. But you've got a chance to get over those fears. Nelson can help you, I know he can. He's a godly man and he's your friend."

"His sermon tonight seemed straight for me."

"It was for all of us."

"Yeah."

The snow dropped softly. Jenna touched Rem's elbow, and he faced her. "We both know you're still a believer," she said. "Maybe it's time you admitted that."

Rem looked at the ground, almost white from the heavy, wet snow. Afraid she'd said too much, Jenna removed her hand. Rem shifted his feet, and she could feel the battle going on in his spirit.

"It's hard," he said softly.

She touched him again. "I'm your friend," she soothed. "Nelson and Julie too. We care for you."

He shivered and shook his head. She waited again.

"I'm afraid," he said. "I don't want to lead you on that I'm different all of a sudden when I know I might never be."

"I'll take that chance," she said. "I believe there's good in you, maybe more than you know."

"I don't want to hurt you," he said. "Like Carl did. Don't want to disappoint Nelson. Don't want . . ." He stopped.

"What?"

"Don't want to come back to God and then fall away again. If that happens, I'll never get back. I know that."

"God gives us lots of chances," she said. "People fall all the time, like bowling pins. Something knocks us down, God picks us up. Something knocks us down, God picks us up."

"You really believe that?"

She nodded. "Yes, I do."

He pulled his hands from his pockets, and she waited one final time. Snow fell into her hair, and she shivered again. Suddenly, he opened his arms. "Come here," he said.

She rushed to him and he hugged her, and she snuggled into his jacket, her arms tight around his back.

"I sold my program," he said.

"Good," she said. "No reason anymore for you to rush off."

"I don't have much money," he said.

"How much is not much?"

158

He laughed and looked into her eyes. "You looking for a rich man?" he asked.

"I'm looking for a warm one," she said. "And I'm not talking about the weather."

He pulled her closer. "I can stay a while longer," he said. "At least long enough for a bike ride or two."

She laughed and he bent to her, his eyes gentle.

"You think you remember how?" he asked.

"I'll do my best," she said.

He kissed her as the snow fell, and she shivered again, but this time it wasn't because of the cold.

∞12∞

A warm sun splashed through Jenna's bedroom window and over her face as she opened her eyes the next morning. She thought instantly of Rem, and a smile creased her mouth and she stretched and almost purred. They'd gone back to his house after they left the cemetery, and Roscoe had served them hot chocolate and a piece of the apple pie he'd bought at one of the sales to raise money for Mickey. They'd talked long into the night, the conversation flowing freely, more easily than she'd ever talked to anyone.

Her phone beeped, and she glanced at the clock. Almost nine thirty. Caller ID showed her mom's number. Jenna's smile vanished momentarily, but she quickly shook off the negative feeling and took the call. Nobody could spoil her humor today, not even her mom at her worst, and on Christmas she surely wouldn't approach that.

"Good morning, Mom," she said.

"What happened to you last night? I close my eyes to

pray and you're gone when I open them again? Then I called you until 1 a.m."

"I went to Rem's house; we talked a long time."

"He'll break your heart. That's all I have to say."

Jenna almost made a smart remark, something like "It'd be a miracle if that's all you have to say on anything," but once more she fought her instinct. "I'm willing to risk it," she said instead. "It's been years since Carl, and even though I don't have a clue if anything serious will happen between Rem and me, it's a chance I'll take."

"He's just like your father."

"No, Mom, he's not, and I'd prefer you not say that again. Besides, Dad's a good man at heart; sure, he's goofed up, but he's no worse than the rest of us. I wish you'd see that."

"He wasn't good to me."

"We all have our failures, me . . . you."

"Are you blaming me for what your father did?"

Jenna got out of bed and walked to the window. At least four inches of snow covered the ground, enough to make everything beautiful but not stop anyone from getting around. Perfect.

"I'm not blaming anybody, Mom," Jenna said. "That's a resolution I've made. I'm going to listen more and judge less. Maybe we should all try that."

Her mom hesitated, and Jenna decided to move things to a more positive tone. "Can we sit together at church?" she asked. "Like always."

The offer seemed to brighten her mom's mood. "I'll be there at 10:45. Will Mr. Lincoln want to sit with you?"

Jenna hesitated. "I don't know if he's coming," she said. "Is it okay if he sits with us if he does?"

Margaret sighed, and several seconds ticked off. Jenna held her breath. If her mom wanted, she could make things really difficult.

"You like this man, don't you?" Margaret asked.

"Yes. He's got a quality about him. You'll see it too if you give him a chance."

Margaret grunted. "You know I just want what's best for you. Your happiness is at the top of my list."

"I appreciate that," Jenna said. "And I'm not sure what the future holds. But that's not the worry right now. I want to take one day at a time; that's what I'm doing with Rem, and I'd like your approval, I really would."

Margaret hesitated one final time, and Jenna knew she was weighing her options. Stand firm against Rem and risk losing her daughter or relax, at least a little, and see what happened.

"Bring him to church if he'll come," Margaret said. "If you're going to see him, I better get to know him and take his measure."

"You'll charm him, I'm sure."

"Don't get sarcastic with me." The words sounded sharp, but Jenna heard a light humor in them. A good sign.

"He'll charm you too; he's got a way about him."

"Like I said, he's just like your dad."

"See you at church."

"Okay, I'll save two seats."

Jenna hung up and moved to the kitchen to make some tea. She had a lot to do this morning. As she turned

163

on the stove to heat water, her phone rang again. She answered and heard Rem on the other end.

"You up?"

"Yeah, a little while ago."

"You want to eat lunch with me and Dad? He said having you here sure brightened up our place."

"I've got church," she said.

"Again?"

"Yeah, it's crazy, but our folks always gather informally on Christmas Day for coffee, cinnamon rolls, a short devotional. It's like family casual and real short. Mom said you could sit with us."

"You got her permission?"

"It took an act of the United Nations, but yes, I did. You better come too, since you made me miss the end of last night's service."

Rem chuckled. "I hope I get credit for going to church twice in twenty-four hours."

"I don't think it'll help you with the Lord, but with Mom, it's a big plus."

"What time?"

"Get there about eleven. We have refreshments, sing a couple of carols, then Nelson gives his devotional. All the children gather at the front with him. We're in and out in forty-five minutes."

"See you there."

"I'm glad you're coming."

Rem sat at the end of the pew, Jenna beside him, Margaret to her right, Roscoe beside her. Although Jenna was surprised to see Roscoe, it had lifted her heart when he'd walked in with Rem, and even more remarkably, her mom had actually smiled when she saw him. Would the miracles of this Christmas never cease?

They'd already eaten their cinnamon rolls, talked with friends, and shared carols. It was time for the devotional. Close to twenty children had gathered on the floor around the stool where Nelson sat. He wore a red pullover sweater and navy slacks. The children's faces glowed with expectation. Pastor Nelson always told the best stories at Christmas.

"I've got a surprise for us this year," Nelson said. "I think the best surprise ever."

Jenna leaned forward. Nelson's expression seemed odd today, like he knew something nobody else did and it pleased him greatly. He picked up a sack from beside the stool and pulled out a handful of cloth masks.

"I want you all to put on one of these," he said, handing out the masks. "Then I want everyone to close their eyes. All of you children and the rest of the congregation too."

He looked up as the children tied their masks on and indicated to everybody to close their eyes. Jenna glanced at Rem, who shrugged and then shut his eyes; she did the same. The children rustled a few more seconds as they got their masks in place. Then they grew quiet. Jenna heard a door open and close. There was the sound of light footsteps, a rustle of clothes, a murmuring as if someone wanted to speak but didn't quite know how. At least a minute passed.

"Okay," Nelson said softly. "Everyone can open their eyes now."

165

The congregation gasped as they looked up. Nelson wore a hospital gown, rubber gloves, and a mask. In his arms he held a baby, also in a mask. Tom and Brenda Strack sat on the front pew close by, their faces likewise covered.

"All of you know little Mickey," Nelson said, holding him close. "I can't let you touch him, because he might catch something from you. That's why we all have on the masks."

The congregation held their breath. What was this about?

"We've all prayed for Mickey," Nelson said. "For his mom and dad too, and his sister, Tess. We want Mickey to get better; we've raised money to help pay for his medical treatment, taken up offerings, left baskets all around the church to receive donations. We've done this hoping he could get an operation to give him a chance to grow up strong and healthy. As I said last night though, it's been hard and things have looked bleak. We've needed a miracle but haven't gotten one. We've all wondered why not. The lack of a miracle has tested our faith and made us cry out to God."

Nelson stood and held Mickey up where the congregation could better see him. The people sat on the edge of their seats. Jenna thought she saw a glistening of tears in Nelson's eyes.

"Today I have good news." Nelson choked. "Last night we got our miracle. I didn't know it at the time, but it came."

The congregation gasped. What did this mean? Had the doctors pronounced Mickey healed? But how? The hospital had sent him home. He wasn't even with a doctor last night. How could a healing have happened, much less been verified?

Jenna wondered if Nelson had fallen prey to some terrible hoax.

"The church treasurer," Nelson explained, "he came to me right after the service. Said he collected the offering baskets sitting around the church at about midnight. One of the baskets contained a check, a big one."

The crowd gasped again. "Two hundred fifty thousand dollars," Nelson said. "Designated for the Mickey's Miracle Fund."

Somebody clapped, and before Nelson could say anything else, the congregation stood as one and began to applaud. Tears ran down Nelson's cheeks and Jenna's too, and when she turned to Rem, she saw his cheeks wet as well, and then everybody cried and hugged and shouted together. People surrounded the Stracks. Jenna wanted to move to them also, but too many people separated her from them, so she just stayed in place and hugged Rem, then her mom and Roscoe too for good measure, the tears pouring down. It took several minutes for the commotion to calm enough for Nelson to call for quiet once more. As he did, Jenna's mind moved to the big question that she suddenly knew everybody wanted answered. Who? What person had acted so graciously? Who had given the two hundred fifty thousand?

Nelson handed Mickey to his mom, then held up a hand to quiet everyone again. "I know what you're asking," he said. "Who's the donor?"

The congregation nodded. Nelson threw up his hands. "I can't tell you!" he said. "The donor requested anonymity, and we have to honor that. Fact is, I don't even know. Only our church treasurer does, and he's bound by law to keep it quiet. So let's just say a prayer of gratitude to God, offer our blessings upon the kind person who did this, and let it go at that. We've truly seen a miracle in Hilltop this Christmas, so let's be thankful." He lifted his arms toward heaven. "Pray with me."

Many in the congregation also lifted their arms. Others knelt where they stood. Tears still filled many eyes. Rem took Jenna's hand and squeezed it. As Nelson began to pray, Jenna kept guessing. Who gave the money? Since she was chair of the group to raise it, could the treasurer tell her? But why did it matter? It didn't, not really. Still, she wanted to know. Who had that kind of money? Nobody she knew, that's for sure.

Nelson finished his prayer, dismissed the congregation, and hustled out with the Strack family. After a few minutes of excited chatter, the congregation rushed out, anxious to tell others what had happened.

Still stunned, Jenna followed Rem out, told her mom she'd see her shortly, waved good-bye to Roscoe, and stood by Rem's car, her mind swirling.

"Who you figure gave the money?" she asked Rem.

"Does it matter?" he asked. "Just accept it and move on."

"But I want to know," she insisted. "Don't you?

He waved her off. "Not if the person wants to stay anonymous. Come on, let me take you home."

She faced the church, its white steeple and the snow-covered ground around it in stark contrast to the blue sky above. "It's a fabulous day," she said. "Maybe the best day ever."

"I agree. Now let's go eat." Rem climbed into his car, and she followed.

As she opened the door, she saw him grab something from the passenger seat and stuff it into his jacket pocket. "What's that?" she asked.

"Nothing." His face turned red.

"What is it?"

"Don't be so nosy."

"You already keeping secrets from me?"

He pulled a brown checkbook from his pocket. "It's a checkbook," he said. "I didn't want you looking in it. I bought you something and didn't want you to see what it cost."

She smiled. "Was it expensive?"

"You'll find out later. Think you're worth something expensive?"

"Do you?"

He chuckled and drove down Main Street. Covered with snow, the town looked like a postcard. She moved to snuggle closer to Rem but then stopped as a series of images popped through her head—Rem crying at the hospital as he held Mickey, his declaration that somebody needed to do something, then last night at the cemetery by his little brother's grave—a brother who'd died of a disease similar to Mickey's. Plus, he'd recently sold his software program. Could it be? She eyed him suspiciously, but he stared straight ahead.

"You wrote that check for Mickey, didn't you?" she asked.

"You're addled," he said.

"You gave it after you heard Nelson's sermon."

"You need medication."

"Let me see your checkbook."

"No way. That's private."

"You have enough money to give away two hundred fifty thousand?"

"Of course I don't. I cleared less than seven hundred thousand from selling my program. I can't afford to give away a third of that to some kid I don't even know."

"It's not a matter of what you can afford," she said. "It's a matter of how kind your heart is. And yours is kind, whether you want to admit it or not."

He stayed firm. "Think what you want," he said. "But don't go offering your theory to anybody else. They'll think you've gone over the edge."

"Not once they know you."

"You figure I'm staying around long enough for that to happen?"

"If I have anything to do with it you will." She kissed him on the cheek. "You're a sweet man," she said.

"Don't let that get around."

"It's our secret," she said.

"You think you're pretty smart, don't you? Maybe you are, maybe you aren't."

"I'm blessed," she said. "That's better than being smart."

Rem drove through Hilltop and up the mountain toward her mom's house. Jenna settled back in the seat. She knew that folks would talk about Mickey's Miracle for a long time, maybe as long as she'd live. But she knew that lots of miracles had happened that year, far more than anybody else would ever realize. That didn't bother her though. She knew, and that was more than enough.

"What do you want to do after lunch?" she asked.

"I thought we might take a bike ride." He smiled mischievously.

"You men are all alike." She smiled back.

"No, I mean a real bike ride—wheels, pedals, gears."

"No, you don't."

"Yes, I do."

They both laughed, and the snow sparkled against the bright sun. Jenna held Rem's hand, and the whole world seemed full of joy.

Gary E. Parker is the author of nineteen published books, including *Secret Tides* and *Fateful Journeys*. He currently serves as the senior pastor at First Baptist Church in Decatur, Georgia, and is a popular speaker on college and seminary campuses. He lives in north Atlanta.